# Praise for Brierley

In <u>WHITE HORSE, RED RIDER</u>  Brierley's writing is so vivid I felt I was there. His words paint a picture that transports the reader to that time and place. After 30 plus years working with writers developing scripts, I have known few who can translate vision to screen. Brierley is one of those few. I love everything he writes.

--- Gay Gilbert, Producer

<u>WASICHU </u>is a remarkable tour de force, bold in concept and brilliant in theme. An excellent read of what the West has become."

---Clive Cussler

<u>TIMELESS INTERLUDE AT WOUNDED KNEE</u> is one of those  wonderful books that is read in one sitting -- not because it has little to say, but because it's said so well that it's hard to put down. The book is so well researched that Brierley's Lakota Sioux leap to life in the reader's eye as they face their darkest hour."

--- The Writer's Showcase

In  <u>YESTERDAY'S  BANDIT,  (Butch  Cassidy's Pursuit of Life and Honor</u>) I believe that Brierley has captured Butch Cassidy's true character. It is a fun read for young and old.  I especially encourage the younger generation to read this book to help give them insight about morals, justice and family values.

---Bill Betenson,
Great nephew and researcher of Butch Cassidy

# WHITE HORSE, RED RIDER

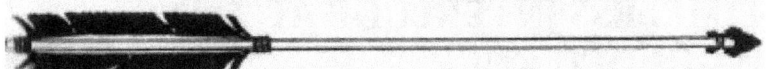

# ALSO BY BARRY BRIERLEY

WASICHU

WASICHU'S RETURN

TIMELESS INTERLUDE AT
WOUNDED KNEE

YESTERDAY'S BANDIT ( BUTCH CASSIDY'S
PURSUIT OF LIFE AND HONOR)

SPIRIT  RIDERS

EDGES  OF  TIME

BASS REEVES, AN AMERICAN HERO

# WHITE HORSE, RED RIDER

### By Barry Brierley

B. BRIERLEY

BEAR BOOKS PUBLISHING

**Manufactured in the United States of America**

**Cover art by Barry Brierley**
**Designed and illustrated by Barry Brierley**

brierleybarry@yahoo.com

*This is a work of fiction. Names, characters, places and incidents are the product of the author's imagination and are used fictitiously.*

ISBN: 978-0-93-302549-3/09-3-302549-1

Published by
**Bear Books**
111 E. Main Street
Florence, Colorado 81226

10  9  8  7  6  5  4  3  2

# CHEYENNE, WYOMING
## JULY 4, 1886

The Cow-town sprawled like a blemish on the undulating skin of the prairie grasslands; it still wasn't much to look at but it was growing. Cattle was the town's ticket to progress, and the Union Pacific Railroad was its vehicle for doing so. It had become a good, clean town, nothing like its early roots when it was known far and wide as 'Hell on Wheels.' The nickname derived from the fact that some of the shacks, saloons, and dugouts were rigged with wooden wheels. This was done to enable the buildings to be loaded back on the train and transported to some other needy depot.

A tall man stood on the edge of the town's main thoroughfare, Sixteenth Street, a wide street running east and west. The man was a rugged, well dressed individual with a lot of years behind him. He stood straight and weather-beaten like a strong old tree, a patriarch of the forest that had survived many storms and through the passage of time had been honed and shaped into a tough, rigid pillar of wood. The man was molded from similar matter. Challenge, hardship, and other adversities had made him the formidable person he was. Many a young cowboy had found out that the years on the man's shoulders had only added to his toughness and his ability to deal with any situation.

He stood beside the unusually quiet street and, as was his habit, first looked to the west, then north. In the west, the mountains were a narrow, blue line with a jagged top edge that reached across the whole flat western horizon. Looking north, it was a different picture; his gaze looked past the reach of the town where the country opened up into rolling prairie as far as the eye could see.

With customary caution the old man hesitated. Before he would step into the open and cross an empty street his eyes relentlessly searched, seeking for danger or anything else that didn't fit the town's normal picture. His gaze automatically followed the line of telegraph poles as they meandered up the wide street. To his aging eyes that had seen so much, they still looked out of place in the west. He looked from the Richardson Brothers' Cafe and Bar on the corner of Ferguson, to Tritch's Hardware on Eddie and Seventeenth. Across the street was the false-fronted Wong's Laundry, and further up Sixteenth, perched a few doors down from the First National Bank, was the impressive three-story Interocean Hotel. Everywhere he looked each and every one of the street's buildings was draped with red, white, and blue banners, commemorating the country's 110th year of freedom.

Beneath the sweep of his moustache a smile appeared. He savored most of the changes in his town, yet liked to remember those first wild years after the railroad came through. The Union Pacific railroad put the town on the map and it was cattle that kept it there. It was during those early years that the town had picked

2

up the 'Hell on Wheels' nickname. Back then gambling, whoring, and killing arrived by rail. The gambling and wenching was brought in for those hardy souls who laid the track and for the local cowboys and ranchers. Also included were all the other men who arrived with hopes to benefit from the service the Union Pacific provided. The killing just naturally followed the rest. Gunmen, gamblers, and crooks were inevitably drawn to wherever men were willing to risk throwing their money away, or take a chance on the turn of a card, or catching a dose of the French pox. Although many thought the old west was on its way out, there were still plenty of reminders that its death would be a slow one.

Sixteenth Street was quiet after the Fourth of July parade; the majority of the town's people had gone home. It was a hot day and most of the street's movement came from a lone dust devil that moved down Sixteenth until it hit Hill Street where it vanished, only to appear again on Fifteenth. Many of the town's residents were spending some quiet time in the shade to escape the heat; only the city park, restaurants, and the saloon establishments flourished.

Moving slowly, the old man stepped into the street and started across. Dressed in a formal black suit he still cut an imposing figure. In the shadow beneath the wide, flat brim of his gray hat, pale eyes watched and saw everything. Leaving his right hand free, he used his left to loosen his tie and the top button of his collarless white shirt. The weathered hand paused just long enough to smooth the double sweep of his gray handlebar moustache. A rollicking version of the song, "Oh, My Darling, Clementine," could be heard coming from a saloon down the street. While in contrast, up the street at Monkey's Oyster Restaurant, a violinist's rendition of "Silver Threads among the Gold" could faintly be heard. As he neared the boardwalk, loud laughter and the shouts of children captured his attention.

Just down the street from the restaurant, tucked in next to a shabby little hotel, was a small saloon; loud, raucous laughter and slurred conversation drifted through its battered half-door. An old, drunken Indian was sprawled out front on the edge of the wooden veranda. In spite of the heat a tattered blanket was wrapped around his spare frame. A handful of boys had formed a half-circle facing the pitiful drunk. Each of the four boys had a willow switch, brought with them from Crow Creek. They were alternately poking and tickling the old man with their supple branches. Drunk as he was, the old Indian was still able to muster a remnant of self-pride and was attempting to ignore their cruelty.

A long shadow crossed between the boys and their victim. As one, they looked up from their mischief and gaped at the tall intruder. The oldest boy, Wes McBride, was their natural leader and spokesman, cautiously grinned up at the old man and said, "Howdy, Marshal. We weren't doin' nothin' wrong, we was just hoorayin' this smelly Injun."

When the town marshal failed to react to Wes' remark, the boys exchanged worried glances. Wes, always the charmer, grinned once again as he asked, "Somethin' wrong, Marshal?"

The old marshal stepped forward, leaned over and braced his hands against his knees. It was a maneuver that put his tanned and creased face about twelve inches from the freckled features of thirteen year old, Wes McBride. Within the deep shadow of his hat brim, the marshal's penetrating eyes locked onto Wes. The boy paled just enough so that his freckles appeared to grow bigger and darker. He dropped his gaze from the marshal's burning stare. Within the shade provided by the drape of the suitcoat, the burnished surface of the five-pointed star winked at Wes. He absently read the inscription incised into the badge's surface, CITY MARSHAL, CHEYENNE, WYOMING. It was a grim reminder of the old man's authority and gritty reputation. Wes was fully aware that, although gettin' on in years, the marshal still had a fierce reputation as a lawman. When he was sober, Wes' pa had told him some stories that near curled his hair. Just last month his pa had said, 'That old marshal ain't never backed down from no one, not ever.' While not having a reason for being frightened, Wes did feel very alone and vulnerable.

"Tell me, Wes, why do I get the feeling you think I'm nothing but a soft-brained, old coot?"

Behind the marshal, Wes saw the half-scared faces of his friends watching him with big eyes. Wes, accomplished liar that he was, said, "Honest, Marshal, we don't mean nobody no harm. That old Injun, he ain't human anyhow. My grandpap, he said once that an Injun ain't no more than an animal that walks on two legs."

Not taking his eyes off young Wes, the marshal slowly straightened.

Noticing the disgusted expression on the old marshal's face, Wes misinterpreted his look for one of agreement. He saw him glance the Injun's way, as if to confirm the animal theory. When the marshal's angry eyes abruptly turned on him like a pair of gun muzzles, Wes knew he'd misjudged the old man and decided it was time to be seen and not heard. The old man swung around and glared at all the boys before declaring, "I think it's time I had a talk with your folks."

All four boys, fearing even a remote possibility of family retribution, started talking at once. Wes thought briefly how his old man would jump at any excuse to give him a whipping.

The old marshal raised a gnarled hand for silence; when it came, he added, "Somehow you boys never got the true picture of Indians. Did you know that most Indian tribes started out being friends to the white man? Most of the Plains tribes were an honest, trustworthy, and friendly people.

At first, Wes was the only boy who showed doubt, although the city marshal was sure that the others had their disbeliefs also. Make no mistake, he thought, Wes was a doubter. Knowing the rough family life Wes McBride had to put up with, the marshal had a tendency to give the boy a friendly hand whenever the opportunity arose.

The boys looked with undisguised disgust at the rheumy-eyed old Indian.

Oblivious to it all, the Indian leaned against one of the saloon's support poles and shut his bleary eyes.

Belligerently, Wes swung his freckled face toward the marshal. After jerking a thumb in the drunk's direction, he asked, "Even him?"

Wes wasn't able to see the marshal's face too clearly because of the shadow from his hat, but he saw him slowly nod, and heard his unbelievable answer.

"Even him... boys, you shouldn't be too quick to judge a man. He may have been a great man in his day. Life is hard. We don't know what misfortune, if any, has turned him into a drunk. And that's the whole point ... we don't know."

No longer quite so afraid of the marshal, one of the boys, a towhead named Johnny, jeeringly exclaimed, "But that's just an Injun!"

Ignoring the fact that some of the boys' folks probably felt the same as their off-spring, the old marshal said, "Tell you what. I won't tell your folks about this here bad doings if you'll listen to an old Indian story I have to tell."

The boys looked at each other. They didn't speak up right away but the marshal could see the excitement building in their faces. Of course it was Wes that made the decision.

"Is there fightin' and killin' in the yarn?" He asked.

"That there is, boy. Back in them days a body had to kill to stay alive."

Wes grinned at his friends, who, taking that as a sure-fire 'yes,' began talking at the same time. The marshal held up his hands to slow them down and added, "Whoa. I think we'd best move on down the street to some shade. Wilkin's General Store's got benches out front."

While they walked, the marshal's gaze habitually swept the streets and the boardwalks making sure nothing unlawful was going on in his town. All the way to the store, the boys cavorted around the marshal like a litter of puppies. Once the boys settled onto the benches and their eyes were watching his every move, he began.

"Have you boys heard tell of how, many years ago up north, trappers used to make a living trapping beaver for their pelts?"

The boys each nodded. Wes added, "Mountain Men."

The marshal bobbed his head, saying, "That's right. Well this here is a story about a trapper who needed a stake and the only beaver around anymore was up in Blackfeet country. The demand for beaver was long gone, so it would take a heap of furs for him to do any good. In those days the Blackfeet were the meanest, most fierce Indians God ever created. He'd been sneaking in and out of their country all winter trapping their beaver. Like a damn fool, he worried he didn't have enough prime beaver and was determined to make one last trip into their mountains before spring set in. Things were already thawing some down on the prairie, but it was still winter up in the mountains. He started out in the middle of a snow storm, thinking there would be less chance of being seen. Not only was he seen, he came mighty close to losing his hair."

The boys had settled down and were all eyes and ears as he continued his story.

"It all began when he was leading his horse along a narrow trail that angled up the side of a cliff that started about halfway up the slopes of a pine-covered mountain. The trapper didn't know it, but he was fixing to experience an adventure that would change his life forever ..."

# ONE

He sat slumped: a dark figure on a white land-scape. The snow continued to fall, dusting his long, blond hair and darker beard with white while adding a pristine blanket to the land and surrounding trees. He was inside a small clearing next to a sheer, rock cliff that towered above the tops of the pine and wind-whipped aspen that made up his small, white world.

His upper body tipped forward from the waist, and his arms and legs sprawled in different directions. Except for the dried blood on his weathered face and beard, his appearance suggested the form of a discarded leather and cloth marionette. On the opposite side of the narrow, snow-filled hollow a pair of brown eyes set within a dark hostile face was staring with unwavering intensity at the unconscious, drooping figure.

Curly Hair, a young Oglala Sioux who had yet to be given his warrior name, watched the white man with fear and apprehension. Fearful thoughts galloped through his young mind like a herd of frightened mustangs. He cradled his injured leg and remembered his earlier violent encounter with the hated *wasichu* (white man).

With growing anxiety Curly Hair had allowed his dappled, tan colored pony to pick his own way along the rocky ledge carved from the looming face of the cliff. The trail was so narrow that at times he could have reached out with his right hand and touched the stone wall's cold face. To his left the tops of the tall pine barely reached the height of his ledge. His pony's carefully placed hooves were nearly soundless on the cushioned snow of the trail. Unfortunately, the rapidly increasing snowfall had added a new danger to the other numerous, natural hazards. Because of the snow's density, his visibility was worsening.

In addition to the dangers of the trail was the knowledge that he was alone in the land of the dreaded Blackfeet, several of whom were probably looking for him at that very moment. A smile briefly brightened his youthful face as he recalled the night before when he had sneaked in among their pony herd. His eyes glittered with pride at having stolen the finest horse in their herd. Curly Hair gave his rawhide lead a tug just to be sure that he did indeed still have the Blackfoot stallion. He smiled at his audacity. But with each bend in the trail his foreboding intensified. He had just pulled his blanket tighter to keep out the swirling snow when he guided his pony around a jutting boulder and came face to face with a blanket-wrapped figure leading a horse. Time stood still. In that frozen moment, the young Lakota caught a glimpse of a bearded face and light-colored eyes. It was a wasichu!

Startled, the white man raised his arm; his blanket flapped in the wind like a giant bird of prey. The erratic, unexpected movement caused Curly Hair's pony to stand up on his hind legs in fright and subsequently alarmed the stolen horse so that he tossed his head and jerked on his lead. The rawhide lead fastened to his wrist pulled him from his mount. Curly

Hair's youthful reflexes were so quick that as he fell, he pointed his borrowed musket toward the imposing figure and pulled the trigger. A blinding flare of orange and red joined an ear-ringing explosion; the recoil jerked the musket from the youth's hand. The stolen horse's rawhide lead snapped, freeing him, as Curly Hair's fur and leather clad body crashed onto the top of the pine trees that bordered the trail. He plummeted downward and painfully smashed through frozen pine boughs, dead limbs, and clumps of snow. While being battered to and fro, the sharp scent of pine needles and sap accompanied the splintering and snapping sounds as the final branches gave way. A solid impact to his ankle shot pain up his leg. A blow to his head followed that obliterated his pain and fading awareness.

The mountain man's first sensation was a combination of cold and pain. He snorted and jerked like a horse startled out of a daydream. Awareness brought with it fear; it was an escalating fear. Collecting the remnants of his scattered senses, he felt the stirring of a new emotion, one that was so foreign to him that he didn't immediately recognize it for what it really was ... panic. The near debilitating passion grabbed him by the throat and would not let go! Short of breath, he found it difficult to breath!

The trapper's sudden distress was so powerful that his first reaction was extreme. Terror pushed a rush of adrenalin through his veins with the speed of light; the double stimuli propelled him to his feet. He swayed like a wind-blown sapling and fell back. His bare hands felt the bite of the icy snow until white pain chiseled into his forehead and obliterated all other concerns. The pain, awakened by his sudden activity, struck with the impact of a hard swung ax-blade. Stubborn, he fought off the hammering pain and tried to think.

Finally, the pain and panic lessoned and his mind returned to full function. His arms swept the area to his front and rear, searching. Fighting down his rising fears the trapper stopped his quest and brought his fingers up to his throbbing face. The sausage-like fingers gently probed and explored the ridges and valleys of his crusted features. Terror again reared its ugly head as the man confronted the true extent of his injury. His mind silently screamed ... I'm blind!

Eight feet away dark, hostile eyes continued the scrutiny of the bloody wasichu. The young Sioux watched as the trapper's large hands carefully searched the damaged face. Above the beaked nose the white man's face was a mass of dried, frozen blood. There was a deep, jagged cut across the broad forehead just above the prominent brow. Curly Hair's breath caught in his throat as the bearded face lifted and turned in his direction. The shaggy head with its white cap of snow cocked to one side in an attitude of listening and then turned away. The young warrior silently released his pent-up breath before his rising excitement created some form of noise and revealed his presence to the hated 'hair-mouth.' He cannot see, he thought. Curly Hair was elated. The white trapper is as blind and helpless as a burrowing mole. It was then that the boy noticed something else that set his hopes plummeting like a broken-winged hawk. Still, he thought, if I am wily like the coyote it will not be discovered until after I am gone, or the wasichu was dead.

The injured trapper, Joshua Donner, knew that he was in a very bad situation. He felt the fear slowly envelope his being like honey being poured over a piece of johnnie cake. The mountain man's thoughts couldn't get past the fact that he was blind and was virtually helpless. How in the devil am I going to get out of this alive, he thought. The question burrowed into his brain and laid there, a dormant enigma without any foreseeable hope.

Tapping into his well of inner strength, Joshua slowed his growing fears and made an effort to sort through the problems concerning his perilous situation.

It's bad, he thought, real bad. I got too many miles between me and my camp. Even if by some miracle I happened to find it, he mused, what then? Knowing that there was no one close enough to help him, Joshua felt old man death's frosty breath caress his soul.

Joshua's thoughts turned briefly to his wife, Swift Runner, who was wintering at Fort Whitewater, down on the Missouri. Thank God, he thought, she won't be alone if I don't make it back. When Swift Runner had told him she thought she was with child, he was thrilled. So much so that he decided to take the gamble and try for some Blackfeet beaver. He thought that if he could stay unseen for the last month of winter, he could pull enough pelts out of those virgin mountain ponds so that he and his wife could afford to enjoy the summer waiting for their child. After the baby came, then maybe even head on down to Taos for next winter.

In a sudden burst of futile anger, Joshua cursed his own stubbornness and greed. It was the fact that most of the country had been 'trapped out' that decreed he risk trapping inside Blackfeet country. He knew that the beaver would be ripe for the picking because every mountain man he knew was too afraid of the Blackfeet to risk their hair by trapping there. The thought of all those virgin beaver streams waiting for him up in Blackfoot country had made him as foolish as a young pilgrim, new to the mountains. Even worse, he hadn't started until winter had already arrived.

In an attempt to better analyze his situation, he ignored the biting cold and let his thoughts swing back to the beginning of what got him in the mess he was in. He chided himself for having to make one last trip to recover his traps and newly caught beaver. Step by step he thought the incident through.

Joshua Donner was trudging through what was probably the last snow storm of the season. His timing had been carefully calculated, thinking that the weather might help to keep him hidden from the watchful eyes of the Blackfeet. His string of traps were planted in several ponds on the other side of the ridge; to get there he had to traverse a narrow ledge along a cliff-face. The rocky trail was so narrow Joshua had felt more comfortable leading his horse than riding him. He recalled how he had been carefully watching where he placed each foot when he looked up and discovered that he was close to spitting distance of a horseback Indian. The swirling snow had made it look like magic; one second he wasn't there and in another eye-blink, there he was. The sequence of events that followed had happened so quickly all Joshua remembered was the Indian pony rearing and how he had lunged away from the cliff's edge toward the rock wall. While falling, the Indian pointed a gun at him. There was a bright orange flash and a thunderous explosion. The musket ball hit the wall beside his head and splinters of rock slashed across his face and brow lacerating his skin. He remembered blindly stumbling away from the wall, then nothing. I must have fallen over the edge, he mused.

Joshua's thoughts abruptly returned to the present. Indian? The hackles rose on the back of his neck like the ruff on an angered wolf. His mind raced with the swiftness that only fear can induce. Where is he now? His paralyzing question grabbed hold of him and wouldn't let go ... is he here?

# TWO

Within the confined space shared with the wolf, Swift Runner sat up. The wolf, Heyoka (Clown), growled softly. Swift Runner's hand calmed him. She didn't know what had awakened her. Then she remembered. She had been dreaming, and in her dream her husband, Joshua, was in danger. He was leading his horse through falling snow along a narrow trail that slashed across a rock face. Her breath quickened as it came back to her. There was a flash of orange and red. Joshua was falling! He was crashing through trees, upside down. Abruptly as it came, the vision was gone. She gasped and sucked in copious amounts of frosty air until she had calmed her fears. Knowing that there was nothing she could do to help, Swift Runner fought off her fears and prayed to Wakan Tanka for Joshua's safety.

Because of the storm she had been napping. With the coming of the child far into the future, she was surprised that she had need of more rest than usual. As she thought of her dream and of Joshua alone in Blackfeet country, she cursed her unusual gift. Some things were better not to know.

Ever since she was a young girl, when she had

been captured by the Crow, she had been able to see and sense things others could not. She thought of it as a Gift of the Gods. In this situation, she mused, it could be painful. Her husband was so far away that her immediate help was not possible. Knowing that he was in some kind of danger only increased her worries. It was well that Joshua did not have the same gift. Not long after he had left the fort and headed toward Blackfeet country, she had been forced out of the small cabin they had shared. An important wasichu with a fur company had come to spend the remainder of the winter at the fort and needed their cabin. Swift Runner and Heyoka had been put outside the fort's walls and into a lean-to that had been built for the fort's sled dogs. Only Heyoka's ferocity and her own fighter's courage had enabled them to drive the sled dogs out of the shelter. Her warrior traits were mostly unknown by the whites. At the moment, fear of the wolf was the only thing that was keeping the trapper/trader, Jed Smith, from dragging her to his blankets.

Smith was a troublemaker who was always fighting and drinking. More importantly, he was an enemy of her husband. His lack of respect for others was widely known. Had he been aware that she was with child, the trapper would not have cared. He would still try to bed her. His kind always took what they wanted; they knew and respected nothing but physical force. Jed Smith had no knowledge of her warrior skills. All he cared about was that Joshua Donner was not around to protect his woman. Had he known of Swift Runner's background and her Crow name, Man Killer, he might have had second thoughts.

As a young slave girl among the Crow, Swift

Runner had shown great interest in the many skills and duties that were expected to be learned by the young men of the Crow. In time she was able to secretly practice those skills which had always been exclusively for boys. Swift Runner's tenacity and will to learn earned begrudging respect from the family that owned her. Her natural skill with weapons and a fierce independence gained her immediate respect. As she grew older, those same skills kept the men from her blankets and from taking her as a wife. Winters passed and her skills were polished until she was considered one of the more accomplished warriors and hunters in her band. Because of her beauty there were still those who sought to mate with her, yet none would risk her fury. One warrior in particular had been enamored by her beauty. He Who Rides Alone had tried desperately to get her into his blankets. In time, however, his pride insisted that he give up his quest.

By the time she was seventeen she had killed three men. Two were Blackfeet, one Cheyenne. Both tribes were enemies to the Crow. It was at that time she earned the name, Man Killer. This ability to kill did not go unnoticed by her would-be suitors... nor did the fact that she had unusual powers. Some thought that she could read minds and see things others did not. There were many who feared her; some did not trust her. Eventually, the suitors looked for tamer, more predictable wives.

Although opportunities were many, Swift Runner refused to fight against her own people, the Lakota. She was determined that one day she would return to them, but it had been so long since she was taken she worried that she would no longer be accepted by her real people, the Lakota. Joshua came into her life at a time when her captors were undecided as to what should be done about their former slave, turned hunter and man-killer. Joshua Donner became their solution. When the mountain man arrived asking permission to trap beaver on their land, the elders in the band put their heads together and found a solution. He was allowed to trap beaver on their land if he would take the slave woman with him as his wife.

Swift Runner smiled as she recalled their early relationship. She consented to leave with him only for the chance to leave whenever she wished and return to her real people. Joshua agreed rather than risk offending the Crow and couldn't wait to be rid of her.

A sudden gust of wind blew snow through a narrow opening. The icy particles flew onto her face blowing away her memories of the past. A trapper's shout brought her thoughts back to the problem of Jed Smith. She thought that part of his interest in her was because of Joshua. Her husband had told her that Smith had become furious when he discovered that Joshua, his father a school master, could read and write. Swift Runner had privately decided that a 'school master' must be some type of elder within the white tribe. She did have to admit that Joshua did not travel on the same path as other trappers. Both in actions and in speech, he was different. Joshua read the thin talking skins that he called books. Also, he seemed more sensitive and caring. He even seemed to regret killing beaver for their pelts. Although when angered his rage was like that of a white-tipped bear, *mato* (grizzly), when he was awakened from his slumber.

Wind and snow whistled through the spaces in

the primitive dwelling and caused the Lakota woman to pull her blanket closer and snuggle next to Heyoka's thick pelt. Feeling the warmth her mind began to drift. As soon as the weather broke, she thought, she would have to decide whether to stay or leave to find Joshua. Swift Runner watched the occasional snow flake drift down from above and thought of her husband and how his love had become such an important part of her life. The wolf's body heat warmed her. Her thoughts and worries drifted away with the wind. She slept.

# THREE

Curly Hair fought off the bitter cold that was burrowing beneath his winter skins. The storm's icy fingers were searching for gaps in his clothing with the relentless skill of the Lakota winter god. Ignoring his growing discomfort, the young Sioux continued to watch and study the white man. He was awed by the huge size of the man. His attention was soon drawn to the white man's skin clothing; its style and beadwork was done in Crow fashion. This discovery narrowed the eyes and tightened the lips of the young Sioux. Instantly, the Lakota youth's hatred intensified. The Crow were the hereditary enemies of the Sioux. He glanced again at the man's white skin and was suffused with a rage that was unusual for his tender years.

The year before, Curly Hair had been spending the summer at the camp of some Brule Sioux on the Blue-water River. The band was led by Chief Little Thunder who had a village of approximately two hundred and fifty men, women, and children. During the previous Moon of the Drying Grass (September), while Curly Hair was away hunting with his friend, Hump, a force of six-hundred soldiers led by a General Harney attacked the village. Eighty-six men, women, and children were killed; seventy women and children were captured. The remaining survivors, less than a hundred, escaped, scattering in every direction without food or water. Curly Hair and Hump, having been attracted by the sound of fighting, returned in time to witness the end of the massacre from the top of a hill. It was the first time a Sioux village had been completely destroyed. The impression the slaughter had made on Curly Hair's young mind was considerable.

After recognizing the trapper's Crow-style clothing, the Lakota was confronted with a new paradox. The man was wearing Lakota style moccasins. How can that be, he wondered. He also noted that the trapper had a fringed, rawhide bag painted in a Lakota manner. The bag hung from his neck and shoulder on a broad leather strap and rested on his left hip. On his right was a powder horn and bullet pouch. At the very moment of this discovery, the huge wasichu again made a sudden movement, rising up onto his hands and knees.

Startled, the Sioux boy became as motionless as a tree. He stared at the white man's strange colored hair and beard. It is like the yellow sky, he thought, after Wi (the sun) has completed his journey. Snowflakes touched his upturned face with icy fingertips and brought his attention back to where it belonged. He watched the trapper slowly shake his head then stop. The shaggy, sightless head turned until it faced him, then stopped and listened. Cold air slipped inside the boy's hunting shirt; a silent shudder racked his slight form. He remained absolutely motionless as the hated one again pushed his hands into the surrounding snow. Slowly he moved his arms in an ever widening arc. The hands, which were turning blue with the cold, were reaching, seeking something unknown.

All at once, Curly Hair saw what it was he was searching for; less than an arrow's length away from the trapper's right hand, a portion of the brass and wood stock of a rifle was sticking up through the snow. As the wasichu's hand moved closer to the rifle, the young Sioux instinctively edged backward. In shifting his weight, he brushed against a snow covered deadfall. A clump of snow fell creating a slight noise.

Hearing the unexpected sound, Joshua, with swiftness not common in such large men, leaped to his feet. With arms outspread, he crouched and faced the subtle threat. With fear of the unknown clutching at his throat, he listened and heard only the rasp of his own breath as he waited and tried to mentally prepare himself for death.

Although still at least six or seven feet away the wasichu seemed to loom over young Curly Hair like a grizzly about to engulf his prey. While his heart threatened to explode with each thunderous beat, the young Lakota clutched his knife as though it were about to leap from his hand.

Head up and once again cocked in an attitude of listening, Joshua took a hesitant step forward.

A jolt of fear propelled the Sioux to his feet. Unable to stop it, a strangled cry escaped his lips as his weight came down on his injured ankle. The unexpected pain made his head spin and sent him sprawling into the snow once again.

Hearing the muffled exclamation, Joshua reactively went into a defensive stance. His remaining senses tried to locate the noise-maker's position while his fear silently screamed, 'Come on... let's get it over with!'

He knew that it had to be the Indian from the trail. Who else could it be? There can't be more than two fools dumb enough to be out and about in a Rocky Mountain snow storm. His musing calmed him. He knew with morbid certitude that the Indian wasn't a Blackfoot. If he was a Blood or a Piegan, Joshua was certain he would be dead by now; 'gone under,' as his trapper friends liked to say. Conceding to his obvious helplessness, Joshua slowly straightened and forced himself to relax. He sat down in the frigid snow and awaited his fate.

Less than half a dozen feet away, Curly Hair relaxed his grip on his knife. He warily watched as the white trapper calmly crossed his ankles Indian fashion, rested his forearms on the points of his knees, and tipped his face upwards as though welcoming the wet touch of the steadily falling snow. The young Lakota watched the wasichu's bravery with unabashed admiration. The white man's courage gave him an idea. He mulled it over and thought that his plan just might work. He studied the mountain man as he refined his scheme. Satisfied that it could work, a grin lightened his dark face and exposed his boyish good-looks. Although fleeting, his smile was as bright as sunlight reflecting off metal. Perhaps, he thought, after using the wasichu's strength to help him escape from this twice cursed country, there will be an opportunity to kill him and take his golden hair. It would only be fitting, he mused, if the first man I kill is one of the hated hair-mouths.

# FOUR

Seven indistinct forms moved across the mountain and winter landscape. Because of the snowshoes tied to their moccasined feet, the Blackfeet warriors' strides were a mere parody of a man's normal walking gait. Each step had to be a reaching, wider stride than normal. All seven Blackfeet blended into their snowy background like the ptarmigan dressed in its winter plumage. Every member of the war party was clothed in a specific fashion to ward off the chill of winter weather and to blend with the terrain. Each warrior was committed to conform to an established code for winter apparel while on a raid or a trail of revenge.

Either a white Hudson's Bay blanket coat or a buffalo robe with the skin side out was mandatory to enable each warrior to merge with the bleak countryside. Some wore fur caps, others used the hood of their capote, but all wore moccasins and mittens with the fur turned inside next to the flesh. Several of the seven warriors carried a small pack and blanket-roll on their back, plus their various war medicine items.. The pack enabled them to transport their personal needs. A supply of dried meat and pemmican was also carried at the beginning of the war trail. In addition to their main

27

weapons, each warrior had a sharp, heavy-bladed knife and a war club or hatchet. The most usual weapons carried were either a short bow or musket; a few of the more wealthy brought both. The lean, scarred leader of the six was such a man.

The great Blackfeet warrior, Dog Killer, set a swift pace through the falling snow. Because he was the pipe-holder of the war party, it was he who led the others. In strict obedience they followed behind him in single file. While he glided across the snowy ground, he searched the vast whiteness for some sign of the Lakota who had dared to steal his horse. Because of the snow and the worsening weather, Dog Killer had decided to pursue the thief on foot. It was obvious that before the Lakota had gotten very far, he would have to abandon his horses or slow to the point where the war party would catch him. In his heart Dog Killer knew that the pony stealer's greed would not allow him to release his horses. He also knew that soon he would have the pleasure of ripping the liver free from the thief's body and eating it before his very eyes. The war chief's black eyes glittered with malice as he thought of the pain and suffering that he would inflict. His teeth were white on his dark face as he smiled and thought of the man's expression at that special moment when he knew that he was about to die.

The tall warrior stopped and looked back at his war party following in his wake. His breath left his mouth in rhythmic clouds of frost as he signaled his men to stop and rest. His hand unconsciously went to a pouch at his hip. Inside was his war medicine, a carved stone effigy of a war horse. He never went on a raid without having it somewhere on his person.

While on a raid all Blackfeet warriors carried some type of talisman, something they considered as their war medicine. It could be merely a feather or a certain bone. Sometimes it was a weapon; often it was a stuffed bird or animal.

Removing his mitten, Dog Killer rubbed the cold-induced tears away from his eyes so that they didn't freeze and interfere with his vision. He sought to control his breathing while his hand absently stroked the scar tissue that formed a lumpy ridge across his narrow lips. The scar was a lesson learned while removing a dead wolverine from a trap. The animal was dead, but his spirit lived long enough to rake one of its long claws down the Blackfoot's face from right eye to chin. Since that lesson, Dog Killer always killed his prey twice.

His head turned, facing up trail. The falling snow touched his face repeatedly with chilled fingers as he watched and listened. There! He heard the sound again. Hoof-beats, muffled by the snow, were coming toward them from the direction the enemy had taken. The pipe-holder hissed and made his warning whistle. All six of the indistinct figures instantly disappeared into the winter landscape. Their tall leader, eyes fixed on the trail, slowly lowered himself into the snow until he was almost invisible.

A dark form slowly materialized as it left the shelter of the pine. The gray horse's stark black mane and tail were the only things that kept it from fusing with the snowy terrain. When its prancing step brought it opposite Dog Killer, the warrior exploded from the snow with a shout. Startled, the gray horse reared. The Blackfoot leader's bare hand snatched at the broken lead; grasping it, he grabbed the mount's ear in his other fist. At first the horse was terrified, but the pipe-holder's familiar scent and persistent shushing sound were enough to calm him. The other members of the war party gathered around. Dog Killer barked a harsh mouthful of Blackfoot and two of their party moved up trail and down to keep watch.

While the pipe-holder examined his mount's legs for injury, the other warriors put out a loose defensive perimeter. With a final grunt of approval, the leader straightened and again looked up trail. The eagle feather attached to his fur hat spun from the silver swivel clasp as a random gust of wind swept by. A stocky middle-aged warrior, with a white cataract covering one eye, stepped up to Dog Killer and said, "This pony stealer's medicine has turned bad. Let me move on ahead. Perhaps he lies injured on the trail or is waiting in ambush. If this is so, I will flush him out of his little nest."

Knowing that the warrior, Weasel Fur, had little in personal riches, Dog Killer nodded allowing him to forge ahead of the others. The stocky warrior grinned, and noting that the horse's tracks were not deep, swiftly removed his snowshoes. Several of the party called out encouragement to Weasel Fur as he shouldered his willow framed snowshoes and quickly surged up the trail following the pony tracks which were being rapidly covered by the falling snow.

Being ahead of the rest of the war party would give Weasel Fur the opportunity to make first contact with the pony stealer. The occasion was as dangerous as it was advantageous. Instead of acquiring the enemy's horse and weapons he could just as easily wind up dead.

Some raiders are very young. They go along in hope of proving their courage and personal status. Many Blackfeet volunteer for raids or horse stealing parties in hopes of bettering their family's position within the band.

Dog Killer gestured to the youngest member of the war party to come closer. Big, black eyes alert, the boy listened intently as his war leader explained how he was being entrusted with the mission of returning his favorite horse to their village. He was then told to find the warrior, Wolf Chief, and tell him bring his dog, *Makwi* (He Who Never Eats Enough), with extra supplies to their war lodge on the ridge. The boy's eyes widened at Dog Killer's last request.

During raids in winter months it wasn't uncommon for Blackfeet to use their dogs as pack animals instead of horses. Usually the dogs were used for carrying tools, snowshoes, and other supplies. Wolf Chief and Makwi were different; the fierce warrior was not a conventional Piegan. Many thought he was a demon; who else would train a domestic animal to kill and cripple? Makwi was half wolf and was trained to track and obey only Wolf Chief. Some Piegan thought the wolf/dog was an evil spirit sent by their enemies.

Dog Killer waved the worried youngster away and made eye contact with his four remaining warriors. His black eyes gleamed as he snarled, "Now we will run this cowardly Cut-throat into the ground. When captured, I will personally cut out his heart and share it with each of you."

Halos of frosty breath swirled about their heads as grunts and fleeting grins of anticipation answered their pipe-holder's boast. The frosty air carried the muffled sound of the gray stallion's hooves as horse and boy moved slowly down their back trail toward the warmth and safety of the distant village.

# FIVE

Joshua's imagination was trying hard to convince himself that he could smell the Indian, but his raging headache distracted him. He inhaled through his nose. The sharp freshness of the cold air made the small hairs in his nose tingle. Yet, while locked within the sterile fresh-ness, he was still unable to smell the scent he associated with most Indians, the mixture of wood smoke, leather, and grease. Had his thinking been sharper he would have realized that his scent was the same as most Indian's. Knowing that Blackfeet, when on the warpath, habitually rubbed the sap from cottonwood trees onto their skin to destroy their man smell, he was relieved not to be able to smell that disgusting aroma. At the moment, the only scent he picked up was of the nearby pine and his own sweat. With a slowly emerging inner strength, the mountain man was able to quiet his fears. He knew that if he were ever to be with Swift Runner again it would be because of his cunning, not his fighting ability. Joshua decided to take the initiative.

"Washtay, *Ozuye* (Greetings, Warrior)."

His words brought forth a sharp intake of air from almost directly in front of him. Joshua smiled and slowly crossed his arms as though huddling from the cold, when in reality he used the move to disguise his right hand slipping inside his fringed and quilled winter coat. His cold fingers closed over the wooden gripps of his cap and ball Paterson revolver. He knew that if he could get the Indian talking he could get a good enough fix on his where-a-bouts so that maybe one of the five balls from his pistol could find him.

The boy was stunned. The last things he would have expected from the white man were a smile and to be spoken to in his native Lakota. I must be careful with this man, he thought, he may be more clever than he appears.

"*Wachin-ksapa ya, Wasichu* (Listen, white man)."

If Joshua had been a horse his ears would have been pricked, attentively standing straight up. He couldn't believe his good fortune. Lakota, his wife's language, was the only tongue other than English that he could speak. Before he could reply, the soft, husky voice spoke again.

"A mistake has been made. On the trail above, you startled me. My gun fired by accident. I meant no ..."

Sensing the Lakota's indecision, Joshua interrupted.

"Our medicine was bad. Things happen. What brings a Lakota to Blackfeet country?" He asked. An inner voice in his head screamed, 'Forget that you're blind! Show him no fear.'

While nervously massaging his injured ankle, Curly Hair's eyes bore into the white man as he said, "I found a Siha Sappa (Blackfeet) horse. His owner did not want him enough to take good care of him. Now the owner wants him back. At this very moment he and some of his friends are searching for me."

While smiling inwardly at the Lakota's subtle humor concerning his obvious theft, Joshua's mind raced. Stealing a horse from the dreaded Blackfeet was like poking a sleeping mountain lion awake with a sharp stick. It just ain't something you do. He fought down a rising anxiety and tried to think of what he could do. The Black-feet may already be within shouting distance, he thought.

"Lakota, why are you still here? Have you been injured? I cannot see. To escape the Blackfeet someone must be my eyes. How are you injured?"

Joshua paused. The intimidating silence of the snow-covered forest was too much for his frayed nerves. He softly added, "If you cannot see either, we are dead men."

Curly Hair knew that his life depended on his proper handling of the white trapper. His young mind wanted to accept the challenge, but he was hesitant to make the commitment. The hair-mouth speaks Lakota, he thought, and is brave like a warrior... all good signs. Having no other choice, the young Sioux took the gamble.

"Hear me, Wasichu, I am called Curly Hair by my people, the Lakota. I am but fourteen winters, yet I have a warrior's heart. If you will be my legs, I will be your eyes."

Behind the bloody mask, Joshua's hope soared. Releasing his grip on the hidden pistol, another smile crumbled the frozen blood trails on his face as he said, "Kola (Friend), you have just made yourself a deal for a horse, a white horse."

# SIX

The pony stealer's tracks led to a trail that was nothing more than a jagged white scar on the face of a sheer cliff. Only the very tops of the tall pine showed above the twisted, narrow trail. Weasel Fur moved swiftly through the falling snow. He slowed when he came to a sharp turn in the trail. The tracks were all but covered, but it was obvious that something had occurred to make the tracks so muddled ... a confrontation of some kind. Head cocked to the side to see better with his one eye, the warrior studied the residue of the tracks. Among the scuffed and drifting snow, he could see that two horses had moved up trail, away from the Blackfeet. With the new snow he didn't notice that tracks had also come from the opposite direction. The accumulating snow made the tracks difficult to read, so Weasel Fur assumed that only one of the horses had a rider and continued to move up trail. He didn't stop to consider where the other horse had come from.

Shortly after Weasel Fur had moved out of sight, five ghost-like figures approached the sharp turn in the cliff's trail. Their breath created brief white puffs of frost that rhythmically rose above their dark faces and drifted away like smoke through the falling snow. Dog Killer stopped. Behind him, his four companions froze in place. He was at the corner. The snow-covered ground at the sharp turn showed signs of having been disturbed. A bird, about to land on top of one of the pine trees that bordered the trail, spied the intruders and flew away. The Blackfeet leader saw and noticed something out of the ordinary. He moved closer. The tops of several of the trees hadn't accumulated as much snow as their neighbors. Moving to the edge of the trail, Dog Killer peered down. The thick pine boughs and the ever present snow wouldn't allow him to see to the base of the trees and the small hollow within. He saw that several boughs were broken and all were not completely covered with new snow. He listened. All that could be heard was the whisper of an increasing wind. When the tall warrior looked up, snowflakes caught on his long lashes and kissed his dark, scarred cheek with lips of ice. Overhead, dark clouds were moving, shifting, threatening with their ominous presence.

Dog Killer barked a guttural command and gestured toward the tree tops. One of the younger of the four slung his bow and precariously grabbed hold of the top of one of the trees. With the sudden weight the pine arced like a mighty bow, the young Blackfoot had to make a sudden lunge for a nearby tree. He missed and went crashing through the snow-covered branches chased by the spontaneous laughter of his comrades. The pipe-holder, Dog Killer, silenced his warriors with a swift look just in time to hear the final impact of their friend as he hit the snowy bottom of the cliff. A groan drifted upward followed by a shaky confirmation that he'd reached bottom. Grins were exchanged behind the pipe-holder's back as he questioned the youth. Satisfied that his quarry was alive and on foot, Dog Killer wiped the smile off the face of one of his more seasoned warriors by telling him to join his young comrade down below. Leaving him with the problem of his descent and with instructions to relentlessly pursue the pony stealer, the Blackfoot leader set off along the cliff trail at a ground-eating trot. He thought that by staying on the ready-made trail down the cliff-side, he might possibly head the thief off and perhaps have an ambush waiting ... that is if his two warriors managed to chase his running rabbit out of its bramble patch and into the open for the kill.

# SEVEN

They burst into the open with an explosion of snow flying in all directions, leaving behind them several pine lacking their blanket of white. Joshua ran with absolute faith in Curly's guidance. He instinctively knew that if they were to escape the Blackfeet it was going to be a joint effort and that there had to be complete trust between them. Their brief plan was to move straight down the mountain, doing so in a zig-zag pattern whenever the incline was too steep to move in a straight downward run.

Curly Hair rode easily on the big man's back; he adjusted to the rhythm of his strides as easily as he would have a new horse. The wasichu's powerful arms hooked around his legs gave him a stable, comfortable base, while leaving his arms free for whatever need may arise. He was amazed, even impressed, by the man's strength and endurance. If the time comes when I must kill him, he thought, I must use caution.

Between them, they had come up with a simple method of communication. He was surprised by the white man's suggestion that, in case words weren't practical, he should steer him by locking his fingers in the long hair just above each ear. Also surprising was the white man's wish that he carry his rifle, which was

41

presently slung over his willowy back by a leather thong. Disturbing as well was the wasichu's wish that he call him Joshua; he had never called a white man by name, nor spoke to one before. In spite of the white man's show of trust and friendship he knew that the wasichus could not be trusted. Why would this one be different from the others?

Joshua's step faltered, interrupting Curly Hair's musing. He noticed the trapper's breathing was becoming ragged while the clouds of frost from his breath were increasing in number. Running through the snow without snowshoes and carrying him, he thought, had to be exhausting. He wondered briefly what had happened to their mounts. Both he and the trapper had their snowshoes tied onto their horse's back. We must stop soon, Curly Hair mused. He thought again of his divided feelings. After witnessing what the Bluecoats had done at Little Thunder's village, how could this man be so different? Once they escaped the Blackfeet, he reasoned, and I am no longer needed, the trapper will change. One thing was certain, he must not let the white man know the truth about his injury. Perhaps I should kill him, he thought, before he does find out the truth.

After what seemed like a large open stretch, they once again entered an area with trees and underbrush. Joshua could smell the pine. His breath was leaving his open mouth in great frosted clouds when he stopped. In between gasps he breathed deeply. Icicles had formed in his beard and moustache, blood streaked his face and stained his hunting coat, making his appearance that of a walking nightmare.

"Are we out of sight from above?" he asked.

Curly Hair slid off the broad back and hobbled a

few paces up their back-trail and said, "Yes. The Siha Sappa (Blackfeet) are still not to be seen."

He glanced back at the mountain man and his heart gave a lurch as he saw the white giant pawing at his bandage. Before they had left, the Sioux had tied a folded cloth over the man's eyes and forehead saying, 'It is best to keep your wound covered so it will heal.'

Joshua quit fussing with his bandage and slumped into the foot of snow. His head ached. It throbbed with each heartbeat. Steam rose from his body as he sat resting. The snow continued to fall but was beginning to slacken. Curly Hair hopped to his side and asked, "If you wish, Joshua, I will tighten the cloth over your wound."

Saving his energy, Joshua nodded. The young Lakota limped behind him and retied the stained cloth. While he worked he thought how easily he could slit the hair-mouth's throat and jump back out of reach. He could stand quietly in the snow so the wasichu couldn't hear him. Happily, he would watch the life pump from his throat in a steaming, crimson stream.

In one swift, sudden move Joshua stood up. The fringed, rawhide bag anchored on his hip brushed against Curly Hair. With the big man's weight behind it, the light contact sent the youth sprawling into the snow; the impact sent a bolt of pain knifing through his twisted ankle. Curly Hair saw Joshua's coiled body and felt fear saturate his whole body. The mountain man was crouched, facing the direction from which they had come. His head was up, nose twitching as he scented the frosty air. The slim, young Sioux noticed these things while swiftly stringing his horn bow and silently pulling an arrow from its quiver.

"Listen," Joshua hissed.

Curly Hair couldn't hear a thing. The quiet was absolute until a slight breeze softly rattled the bare upper branches of a nearby aspen. He quickly hobbled past the trapper until he had a good vantage point and peered along their back-trail. Their telltale course through the smooth blanket of new fallen snow was a stark reminder of how easily they could be tracked. His almond shaped, brown eyes didn't blink as he carefully scanned the disrupted snow that marked their passage down the mountain. There! He saw a flicker of movement come from a small copse of pine and stunted aspen. Among the trees there was a brief flash of sun-kissed metal, a flutter of feathers, and fur above a dark face. Curly Hair felt a slight twinge of fear.

"*Natan uskay* (Attackers are coming)?" Joshua asked.

"*Han* (Yes). But I see only one."

"Is he coming fast?" Joshua's whisper prompted a head shake from Curly Hair, until he realized his mistake and said, "*Heyah* (No). He is about an arrow's flight up the mountain and is in some trees. Between him and us there is no more cover, just a snowy slope. I do not think he will be in a hurry to cross the open ground."

Joshua's bearded face turned toward the sound of the Sioux lad's voice as he said, "Come, Warrior, you must be my eyes." His whisper crackled with passion. "If this scalp hungry Blackfoot is alone, we must prepare a welcoming surprise for him."

Almost as an afterthought, he softly added, "I don't think they have figured our tracks out yet. It is very important for us to make the enemy think that we are only one person. And, if at all possible, we must kill him without using the gun. The noise would bring his friends as quickly as wolves to the bawling of a lost buffalo calf."

Reaching inside his fringed winter coat, Joshua pulled out his revolver. As his fingers blindly felt for the caps on the five nipples of the gun's cylinder, he added, "But just to be on the safe side, I'll make sure this is ready."

Curly Hair's eyes had widened at the sight of the pistol. This Joshua, he thought, is a man of many surprises. If he has one planned for me, I must be ready to react with the swiftness of the wildcat.

# EIGHT

Swift Runner clasped her blanket coat at the throat and stepped from the lean-to. Once again she looked to the northwest. While she looked she waded through the foot of new snow to the edge of the dog run. The snow had stopped and the air was sharp and crystal clear. Her breath drifted in silvery clouds into the bright blue sky. Everywhere she looked the land was covered with a beautiful, new blanket of white, a gift from the Sky Father. The mountains, although more than a single days ride away, still appeared to loom above. She stared hard at the distant peaks hoping Joshua was all right. Her dream during the storm had been so real that she was frightened. In her heart she knew that if she was to have any peace she must go and find him.

Earlier she had prepared her things necessary for travel. Some of their possessions from the cabin she had left with a friendly Crow family who said they would stay near the fort until late spring. Behind her the activity at the fort was picking up now that the snow had stopped. She began walking toward the river. Her gaze scanned the flat leading to the cottonwoods by the river. Trappers, keel boat men, and muleskinners were preparing their equipment and working with their animals. She veered east toward a secluded portion of the river. In spite of the cold and the icy water, like most of her people, Swift Runner bathed daily. While she walked her thoughts suddenly turned to Heyoka. She was beginning to get worried. He hadn't been around for most of the day. Usually the wolf was so protective of her that he was always close at hand. She stopped and listened. The wind was blowing softly through the trees. She shut her eyes and listened. It was whispering to her.

*"Hola!"* The shout spun her toward the fort. Two trapper friends of Jed Smith were tightening the loads on their pack mules. Both waved and grinned. The one called "Frenchy" swept his red knit cap off and made a mock bow in her direction, shouting, "Hallo, Mrs. Donner! Did you have nice nap?"

He grinned and made obscene motions with his hips. Turning away Swift Runner continued her stroll toward the bare cottonwoods and clumps of pine that bordered the river. Sneaking another glance at the two trappers, she saw they were still watching her. She absently wondered where Smith was; rarely had she seen him away from his partners. Probably setting up a rendezvous, she thought, to sell whiskey to the blanket Indians near the fort. She knew for a fact that the three rarely trapped. Most of their time was spent selling raw whiskey to all comers, mostly Indians. Manuel, the clerk at the fort, had been trying for months to catch them at it. Not out of a sense of outrage, but to keep the commerce for himself and for those who owned the fort.

Moving soundlessly through the snow-laden trees, Swift Runner pulled her blanket capote close about her and slipped down the bank to the river. There was a sharp bend in the river just before the fort's landing, so she was out of sight of those working there. The smell of cottonwood and willow was sharp in the brisk air. As she began to strip she noticed that beneath the snow some of the bushes and trees were starting to bud. The storm probably froze all growth from the greenery, she thought, yet it was heartening to know that spring was on its way. An inexplicable noise brought her head up. Not ten feet away, Jed Smith stood leaning against the white trunk of a cottonwood. Bearded to the eyes, his sneering smile was like a slap in the face. He was openly leering at her nakedness. She still had her elk skin dress in her hand. A buffalo robe was tucked under Smith's arm. Looking into his eyes she knew immediately that it was a planned attack. When Smith's friends had called to her it was probably to divert her attention so that he could slip down here unseen ahead of her.

Smith was a big man, middle-aged. His filthy breechclout, greasy, fringed buckskins and quilled moccasins were a silent declaration that he'd been in the mountains long enough to know that what he planned to do just wasn't done, unless he was willing to fight Joshua to the death, and possibly die for his deed. Unfortunately, in his small, vicious mind, he didn't think he was doing anything seriously wrong.

Many whites, even some of the trappers, thought of Indians as nothing more than another form of wild animal that they could use as they wished.

Swift Runner knew that to stop him now, she would have to kill him. Unafraid, she watched his small eyes devour her body. The way they darted here and there she was reminded of a weasel or ferret. When the beady eyes lifted and met her penetrating black ones, she said, "If you do this thing to me, you are also doing it to my husband."

Jed Smith smiled as he said, "I don't set much store by yer high 'n mighty husband. B'sides ye been askin' ta be mounted ever since he left."

Smith moved in close. Swift Runner could smell his rankness. Her eyes lifted to meet his. When she spoke, her voice was filled with loathing and menace.

"Do what you must. But remember this, wasichu ... I will kill you. Even if you leave, I will find you ... and I will kill you."

For just an instant, Smith's smile wavered. Then he laughed aloud saying, "Ain't no need to go lookin' 'cause I'll be right here. B'sides when I'm done, you jus' might be wantin' ta change stud horses."

Her dress dropped from her hand. Smith's eyes again raked her body. He grinned at her jutting nipples and smiled in anticipation as his gaze swept over her slightly rounded stomach and her long, lean legs. A frigid breeze swept by that started a tremor moving up her legs. As it passed through her body she began to shake. Not once had Swift Runner's eyes left the trapper's face. Her demeanor was so grim her face could have been carved from red sandstone. Slowly her hands raised to her neck. Smith's quick glance saw a tiny gold cross beneath a rawhide choker with a small bear carved from bone. He watched her hands disappear beneath the blue-black mane of hair as though to untie the talisman or cross. Feeling the heat of her gaze, his eyes met her look of ebony fire just as her hands swiftly left the back of her neck. Smith's brain barely had time to receive the message that the necklace was still on her neck before he felt a deep pain rip and tear into his crotch. The buffalo robe fell unnoticed as his hands involuntarily went to the injured area. Immediately, they filled with blood. He opened his cupped hands and stared in absolute horror at the deep, vicious slash across his bunched genitals. His bulging eyes shifted, and he saw the bloody knife clenched in Swift Runner's fist. The image blurred and he felt another searing pain across his throat. Blood gushed down his front in a red flood. Still clutching his ruined genitalia, Smith, his face locked in an expression of horror, dropped to his knees. Swift Runner stepped back. Her eyes swept the area to see if anyone had seen. Smith's eyes rolled her way. A horrible gurgle came from his throat as he tried to speak before toppling forward onto his face, hands still buried in his sodden crotch. He twitched. A long sigh passed his lips as his body relaxed and his eyes stared straight ahead, seeing nothing.

Looking all around to be certain no one had seen, the Lakota woman crouched and quickly cleaned her flat compact knife in the snow and replaced it in the sheath that nestled between her shoulder blades beneath her flowing hair. She quickly adjusted the rawhide choker so that the sheathed knife that was suspended from it wouldn't put too much pressure on her throat.

Moving with great speed Swift Runner got dressed, dragged Jed Smith's body into the bushes, and worked to obliterate the spilled blood that had soaked into the snow. With a final sweep of her moccasin covered foot, she brushed another clump of clean snow over the remaining pink stain and turned up river. She followed the bank of the Missouri as it twisted south until she was behind the fort and away from the eyes of Smith's friends, who were more than likely awaiting his return. Slipping up against the sharpened ten-foot, peeled pine posts of the fort's stockade, Swift Runner quickly waded through the drifted snow until she could peer around the northeast corner. With Smith's friends nowhere in sight, it took her just moments to round up her things and head toward the Crow camp. Visiting the dog run had reminded her of the missing Heyoka. All she could imagine happening was that somehow, Smith and his friends were able to capture the wolf, or secretly kill him. In the past, he had never been away from her side for longer than a few heartbeats at a time. Joshua had spent many suns training him.

Two winters ago, she and Joshua had found the wolf pup lying beside his dead mother. There was no sign of his brothers and sisters. There were plenty of tracks of another adult wolf having lingered nearby, but no actual sightings of him. Even then, as a pup, Heyoka had taken to her first. As her people would say, they have always walked in each other's footsteps.

Near the edge of the Crow camp she found the tipi where her supplies were stored. Removing her coat, she quickly prepared for her journey. Beneath her softly tanned dress, she wore leggings and breech-clout. Quickly she untied the two sides of her dress, so that the sides would be open up to her waist for riding. She then wrapped a wide, red trade cloth sash around her waist and slipped into her white, hooded blanket coat. Swift Runner grabbed the mate to Joshua's Paterson revolver and checked the caps seated on the nipples of the gun's cylinder before thrusting it behind her sash. She then pulled the coat tightly around her middle with a leather and silver concha belt and pushed the brass-studded leather sheath that held her ten-inch Bowie knife to the middle of her back. She hesitated over carrying Joshua's spare throwing axe in her belt. He was the expert with the war-hawk, not her. (Among the trappers and traders in the West, the hand axe was known as a war-hawk, or just hawk. In the East, the very same weapon was known as a tomahawk.) After slipping her beaded, otter fur quiver that carried her horn bow and arrows onto her back, she snatched her packed parfleche and was ready. When she arrived at the pony herd the two small boys in charge called to her. Answering their good natured shouts she looked for her and Joshua's remaining horse.

Needing transportation and a pack animal, Joshua had taken two of their horses with him. That leaves me, she thought, with *Sosa Minne* (Muddy Waters). She smiled, in pleased anticipation.

Made uneasy by Swift Runner's scent some of the ponies in the small herd began to mill around. Plumes of condensation rose from the snorting, nervous mounts. A smallish, dappled Appaloosa saw her and came at a trot. Velvet nose nuzzled her cheek as the speckled horse moved in close and snuffled her hair. His shaggy winter coat had more gray than white, and the black spots that scattered upwards from his knees were of all sizes. Joshua said that if it weren't for the black tail and mane, Sosa would look as though he were a white horse that had run across a large puddle of black mud. Swift Runner knew that the Appaloosa had seen too many winters, but she loved him best. He was a small horse with a big heart.

After saddling up and tying a blanket roll and

parfleche in place, Swift Runner tied a pair of braided rawhide loops loosely around her horse's body. Old habits are hard to ignore, she thought, and mounted up. She made a swing to the west to avoid the fort and pointed Sosa's nose northwest.

Leaving the sight of the ugly fort behind her, Swift Runner relaxed and enjoyed the freshness of the unspoiled air. The mountains towered in the distance. Knowing that Joshua was somewhere in their midst the sight of the purple monoliths crouched on the horizon gave her peace. *Wi* was making a late appearance. She welcomed him as his warmth touched her left cheek. The wind whistled through the trees. She listened carefully. A slight sound from her back-trail pulled her head around. Half expecting to see Smith's two partners closing fast, she was delighted to see the shadowy form of Heyoka lunging through the snow tight on her horse's heels. A white grin lit her dark face as the wolf's muscular form lunged to the left and kept pace on her right flank. Her smile widened when she noted the collar and the long strap of chewed rawhide trailing behind. When she saw the red stains that covered Heyoka's muzzle, Swift Runner laughed aloud, knowing that the wolf-dog had made one of them pay for their cruel treatment.

When they got into open country she urged Sosa to a greater speed. The winds across the open plains had blown much of the new snow away which allowed them to move much faster. She thought again of the day's dream and prayed to Wakan Tanka that Joshua was still alive.

# NINE

    Being careful not to put much weight on his ankle, Curly Hair swept away the last of any telltale tracks and hid himself opposite the single trail they had left for the Blackfoot. After all the effort he and Joshua had put into preparing for the ambush, he was sweating in the chill air. Big, wet flakes continued to fall, but with the lessening of the snowfall visibility was much better. He watched as the warrior cautiously moved into the open. Frost rose from his head like wraiths of smoke. The Blackfoot was tall but moved with the quickness of youth. A fur hat with a feather adorned his head. In one hand was a bow and arrow, a short, heavy war club in the other. A white, striped capote (blanket coat) helped him blend with the terrain. Curly Hair was careful not to stare directly at him. He knew that if the Blackfoot was a seasoned warrior he would be able to feel his eyes watching him. Suddenly the warrior began to run downhill. He stopped so abruptly that his feet slid and he fell. Up in an instant, the Blackfoot sprinted in another direction so that he wasn't a sitting target. He slid to a stop behind a small bush and crouched in the snow, making himself as small a target as possible.

    Movement caught Curly Hair's eye. His heart

began pounding so hard he felt it in his throat ... a throat that was suddenly parched and dry. Fearful that the condensation of his breath would be seen, he tried to slow his breathing. A second warrior had cautiously stepped out of the pine into the open!

The Lakota youth's head began to spin. He didn't know what to do. Fear clutched at his insides with taloned fingers. The wasichu thinks there is only one enemy close by, he thought. How do I warn him? His mind raced in circles like a dust devil as it searched for a solution. Without moving his body, Curly Hair's eyes shifted to where Joshua lay in wait.

A large tree had fallen, its dead branches sprawled in a large, snow-covered canopy. Joshua's tracks crossed over the snow-laden trunk, near where the branches began their outward thrust, and continued on until disappearing into the trees. Following instructions, Curly Hair guided Joshua back to the tree, where he then had hidden in the hollow beneath the trunk and enveloping branches. With a distinct limp, the Lakota had then brushed away all the tracks except the ones that would lure the Blackfoot into the trap.

The two Blackfeet were much closer now, yet were keeping the same distance between each other. Curly Hair carefully breathed into the V-shaped quilled panel at the neck of his war shirt to break up the clouds of frost from his breath. As the first Blackfoot came closer, he saw that he was a young warrior as he had suspected. He didn't appear to be much older than himself. The second one moved more cautiously and with more skill like a mature warrior. Snow had accumulated across his broad shoulders and conical fur hat; three dyed feathers were attached to its front. A wolf skin was tied around his upper body, and a gray blanket was fastened around his waist. The wolf pelt's fur was on the inside for warmth, and its tanned white hide helped him mesh with the snowy background. He carried a short musket in one hand and a heavy-bladed knife in the other.

The young Lakota watched closely as the first Blackfoot neared the edge of the trees. With an arrow already notched on taut, twisted sinew, Curly Hair stared at the hard, youthful face revealed beneath vertical red stripes of war paint. He knew what he had to do. Moving his lips in a silent prayer to Wakan Tanka, he prepared himself.

Staying hidden, Curly Hair spoke in a voice just loud enough for the trapper to hear him. The first Blackfoot was sure to hear also; Curly Hair just prayed that he did not understand Lakota.

"Hear me, Joshua. There are now two warriors, one behind the other."

Holding his breath, the Lakota peeked around his tree cover and through a lattice of thin branches and saw that the first Blackfoot had stopped just inside the trees. He was crouched; looking frightened he was peering in all directions for the source of the voice. Curly Hair spoke again.

"I will try to kill the first one. If I miss I will lure him away. The next will be sure to follow and you can kill him. Be ready. He looks strong."

Making certain that the downed tree was between him and the Blackfeet, Curly Hair quickly hobbled into the middle of the trail. Bow in hand he swiftly pulled the arrow to his cheek. The Blackfoot warrior was frozen in place. At the very instant of the arrow's release, Curly Hair was distracted. The arrow went wide.

The Blackfoot's bow raised. Curly Hair spun around and was taking a full running stride when his bad ankle collapsed. As he fell the arrow hissed by his ear in a loud whisper, an eye-opening reminder that death had been but inches away. Landing face down, he felt the icy bite of snow on his hands and face. He scrambled to his feet. Bow in hand the Blackfoot was running straight toward him and the fallen tree.

Curly Hair's distraction had been movement coming from the hollow beneath the snow-covered tree trunk. Again he hesitated. The sight of Joshua breaking free from the snow that hid him pushed the Lakota into action. Clearly hampered by his bad ankle, he stumbled and hobbled up the snowy trail. Clumsily he struggled to notch another arrow and glanced back just as the lead warrior leaped up onto the tree's large trunk. Having faked the severity of his injured ankle and his clumsiness, Curly Hair stopped, pivoted, and pulled his arrow back. With thumb anchored against cheekbone, his fingers flicked open releasing the gooseberry shaft. The arrow's flight was brief. It hardly seemed to have left the Lakota's ash bow before it buried half its length high into the man's chest. Mouth open, eyes wide with surprise, the young Blackfoot warrior toppled backwards off the log and out of sight.

Behind him the other Blackfoot was running hard. Snow was flying into the air with each lengthy stride. Beneath the garish paint, Curly Hair saw the hate emitting from the dark face. Trying not to fumble, he snatched another arrow from the quiver. The Blackfoot's black eyes were blazing as he avoided his downed companion and vaulted the snow-covered tree trunk.

Eyes still locked with Curly Hair's, the warrior's moccasined feet landed in the snow in front of the tree trunk. Before the boy could notch the arrow on the sinew bowstring, a pair of large hands shot out of the dark shadow beneath the downed tree and clamped around the warrior's ankles, jerking his legs out from under him. The burly Blackfoot's fur hat flew in one direction, the short musket in another. Curly Hair stared in awe as Joshua, snow clinging to hair and beard, exploded into the open, causing snow to fly in every direction. The Blackfoot had landed on his hands and knees and only managed to get one foot under him before Joshua's body slammed into him from behind, driving him into the snow. The big warrior screamed with rage and broke free from the trapper's grip. Before he could get to his feet, Joshua was on him and swiftly buried his war-hawk blade into the center of his head. The warrior stiffened, fumbled at the war club in his belt, then soundlessly crumpled to the ground where he quivered and was still. Joshua bent forward, grasped the wooden handle, jerked the small axe free from the man's head, and straightened up. The horrible wet sound the war-hawk made when it came loose seemed to echo in the quiet of the snowy glade.

Curly Hair's eyes lifted to see the mountain man standing upright facing him. He looked like a winter *kaga* (demon) with his gory head wound, blood-streaked face, snow-covered beard, and buckskins. But what frightened him the most were Joshua's light blue eyes; eyes that were staring straight at him.

He can see! The young Lakota's mind raced.

Now that he can see again, he thought, the wasichu knows that I tricked him! The words seemed to bounce inside his skull until he thought they would leap from his mouth. His gaze drifted beyond the wasichu; shock sent a jolt through his young body. Suddenly, in one fluid motion, Curly Hair brought his bow up, pulled the arrow back, aimed, and released.

Joshua ducked aside as the gooseberry shaft buzzed by his ear. His look behind was in time to see the younger Blackfoot, with arrows sticking from both chest and throat and bright blood spilling over his chin, drop his war club, slide off the snowy trunk, and disappear behind the downed tree.

Caught between having killed his first man and the added shock of the wasichu regaining his sight, Curly Hair's thoughts were in a quandary. With a patience and control far beyond his years, his mind stilled like the fading ripples on a pond as he waited to see what the trap-per was going to do. The large snowflakes that managed to filter through the canopy of branches helped calm his fears as they fluttered to the ground.

Joshua squatted and quickly cleaned the blade of his hand-axe in the snow. He stood and again met Curly Hair's gaze. War-hawk in hand, he walked toward him. The boy's legs quivered as though they had a mind of their own and wished to run. His heart was pounding so hard, he was certain that it would be heard. Joshua stopped directly in front of Curly Hair. His hand slowly raised and reached for the young Lakota.

Although on the outside he didn't move, on the inside the boy's heart flinched, and his hand covertly inched toward his sheathed knife.

Joshua carefully picked up a length of the youth's dark brown hair. Noting the distinct wave, he dropped the hank of hair and absently said, "It seems that blood from the wound on my forehead had frozen and sealed my eyes shut."

The young Lakota watched a plume of smoke-like condensation lift in the still air, then drift away with the last of Joshua's words. Curly Hair waited for the white man's anger he felt certain was forthcoming. The mountain man's bloody face and crimson-edged eyes were frightening enough without having to wait for his judgment. Gesturing at the brown wavy hair, Joshua continued, "Now that I can see again, I understand why they call you Curly Hair." He paused before adding, "I think I will just call you Curly."

At first Curly Hair was angry that the wasichu would call him by his nickname as though he was a friend or relative, but he calmed his anger and waited. It was then, he thought, that Wakan Tanka proved he was watching over me

Joshua smiled, looked into the Sioux youth's eyes, and said, "When you wrapped a bandage over my eyes before the run, it held in the heat from my body. With all that running, I became hot and sweaty. Looks like that's what thawed the frozen blood."

He looked away for a moment. When the trapper's gaze returned Curly Hair was certain that he saw a mysterious glint shining within the blue of his eyes. It was something warm and wondrous, something like friendliness. He didn't know what to think or believe, but he sensed that the trapper was trying to be a friend.

Joshua offered his hand to shake. Dazed by it all,

Curly Hair slowly took his hand. With a quiet sincerity, Joshua said, "Le mita pila, kola (Many thanks, friend). You are a true warrior."

Gesturing toward the Blackfoot beyond the tree trunk, he continued, "I owe you my life. The least I can do to repay you is to continue to be your horse."

# TEN

    With Curly's help, Joshua busied himself trying to smooth out their tracks leading to the tree-covered glade where the killings took place. His plan was to return to the spot where the first Blackfoot had been seen and continue on in a different direction from there. He knew the cover-up wouldn't completely fool anyone, but it would at least use up some of their time and keep them guessing. Joshua noticed how the sky was becoming lighter and the snow was falling with much less intensity. Knowing that if they lasted till nightfall they'd be needing it, Joshua stripped the wolf skin off the dead warrior and handed it to Curly. He grimaced when he saw that the boy had taken the young Blackfoot's scalp and fastened it to his belt. He watched the blood slowly drip into the snow and briefly chided himself for his silent criticism. Joshua knew that once the snow stopped the rest of the Blackfeet would be coming full bore and, being Blackfeet, they won't be satisfied with just taking their scalps; they'll cut off both hands and feet and probably their heads too. Turning away, he got busy preparing for their run. He knew that good fortune and quick thinking would have to be with them if they hoped to get away.

    Settling Curly on his back he began to run. Instead of moving southeast as they had initially done, he began running northeast, deeper into Blackfeet country. Joshua decided to gamble; because of the earlier heavy snowfall the main group of Blackfeet was still not aware of his presence and had continued on along the cliff trail in an attempt to head Curly Hair off. Joshua reasoned that the leader would probably figure that the boy would take the fastest route out of Blackfeet territory and make a bee-line for the protection of his own land. Only time will tell if I'm right, he mused.

He ran hard. This time it felt different, Joshua was filled with confidence. The fact that he could see and that his Hawken plains rifle swung from his right hand probably had something to do with his assurance. Curly was perched on his back; on the boy's back was the wolf pelt and painted, rawhide parfleche with Joshua's 'possibles' and extra clothing. Just the lack of the rawhide bag's bouncing and banging on his hip put a new lightness in Joshua's stride. He wished that he knew how many Blackfeet were chasing them. It would also be nice to know, he mused, if any of the raiders were on horseback.

While he ran, Joshua's thoughts turned to Curly Hair. With his lighter skin and wavy hair, he wondered if there was any white blood in his family. He was fascinated by this unusual Lakota boy. Joshua had never seen anyone with so few years as mature and brave. The boy, he thought, knows how to think on his feet. He knew in his heart that, right from the start, Curly had seen that Joshua's eyes weren't damaged and that he was using Joshua as a tool for his own survival. In all fairness he couldn't really blame him. Having noticed the occasional wary look in his eye, Joshua sensed that he had good reason not to trust whites.

When the terrain finally permitted him to do so, Joshua turned and angled back toward the south. His breathing began to labor until rhythmic puffs of frost were rising with the regularity of a steam engine. Crossing a large tract of open ground, he concentrated on establishing a tempo, a pace that would make each footstep a natural gait. Although swiftly weakening, he forced himself to continue on until they entered a distant copse of pine and aspen. Once inside the protective cover, his strides slowed and stopped. When Curly slid off his back, Joshua stretched, arching his back. His powerful legs quivered with fatigue. He noticed that Curly, after letting the parfleche drop, quickly moved to a vantage point where he could see their back trail. Pleased by the boy's ability to think for himself, Joshua sat down in the snow. He cradled his rifle across his lap and put his back up against a tree. Out of habit, he pulled from his parfleche a dog-eared copy of The Last of the Mohicans by James Fennimore Cooper. There was no time to read but just the feel of the compact volume gave him comfort, as would any familiar object. The laceration across his forehead began to throb and he felt light-headed. He shut his eyes and leaned his head back. Hearing a slight sound, Joshua opened his eyes. Startled, his stomach lurched. Curly Hair was crouched only a few feet away watching him.

"The snow has stopped, Joshua. Rest. I will keep watch."

Joshua noticed how Curly's brown eyes covertly appraised the book before looking away. Too exhausted to reply, he merely nodded as Curly slipped past him and out of sight.

Joshua listened but couldn't hear him move away through the snow. His mind wandered, and he absently wondered how he would explain a book to a boy of Curly's age who had obviously never seen the inside of a school; he stopped when his forehead began to throb. He shut his eyes again. In his mind he saw Swift Runner; she was smiling and walking toward him. In one hand she carried her sinew-wrapped horn bow; a beautifully decorated otter fur quiver of arrows was in her other hand. It was a breezy, summer day and the sun was glinting off her unbound, blue-black hair. A gust of wind caught her loose tresses, sweeping them into the air where they floated like strands of spun silk. As though it had happened yesterday, he recalled how he first learned of Swift Runner's true name and warrior skills. He smiled, remembering.

Several days had passed since Joshua and his new wife had left the village behind them. Neither had spoken to the other except out of necessity. Joshua resented having to marry the slave girl just because he needed to trap on Crow land, and he sensed that the Lakota girl wasn't too happy about the arrangement either. Having wintered with a trapper that was half Sioux, Joshua could speak passable Lakota. His Crow was so bad he wasn't sure he got her name right. Not that his fluency in Sioux had helped their relationship any. On different occasions, he had tried to approach her but always changed his mind at the last moment. It bothered him that everywhere she went, even in camp, she had some kind of weapon with her. He was taking it personal as though the weapons were meant to keep him away.

Late that day they had stopped beside a stream to eat and set up camp. Swift Runner had noticed there were some ripe berries growing across the stream. She pointed them out to Joshua who responded with a grunt and nod. While stripping their pack horse, he noticed that she had untied one of the bundles she brought from the Crow village. Joshua watched as she removed a beautifully tanned fur quiver, brimming with arrows and a graceful appearing, well-crafted horn bow from the leather-wrapped container. Swift Runner slipped the quiver over her head, allowing the beaded strap to cross her chest and rest on her right shoulder. Pulling a woven grass basket free of the bundle, she strode purposefully toward the crossing in the stream.

He stared in disbelief.

"Where are you going?" he asked.

Swift Runner stopped and slowly faced him. As she said, "I am going to pick some berries," she swiftly strung her bow and looked at him. Her face remained expressionless as she quietly watched him.

Puzzled, Joshua shook his head. He couldn't help admiring the picture she made, standing so straight and proud. The sun brought copper highlights from her raven hair and spots of light that glittered in her eyes. It was the eyes that showed him that her patience was nearing its end. Or is she hiding something, he wondered.

"Where did you get that bow?"

Before she had a chance to answer, he added, "If you stole that from the village, will not some angry warrior come looking for his horn bow?"

She stiffened with anger and turned to cross the stream; instead she stopped. Facing him she said, "Do not worry, Wasichu, I will protect you."

As she turned to leave, Joshua shouted, "Wait!"

Swift Runner stopped and again faced him.

"Wonumayin (A mistake has been made)," he said.

She turned to leave.

Quickly, he said, "*Ehunun* (Truly)!"

She stopped.

For some reason, Joshua felt drawn to the woman. Not because of her beauty; it was something else. There was some unknown pull that made him want to please her, or at least have her understand him. He certainly didn't understand her.

"There is something I wish to ask you," he had said.

Her eyes shifted, softened. There was even the suggestion of a smile, as she said, "No. I do not carry weapons to protect myself from you."

Joshua stared. How in the hell did she know that, he wondered.

"Why do you always carry weapons?"

Surprise changed her expression as she replied, "They did not tell you of me?"

He shook his head in confusion.

Mischief was in her eyes as she asked, "Did they say my name?"

Embarrassed, Joshua lowered his eyes. She was waiting, so he said, "I don't speak much Crow, but it was, Man Lover ... or, Lover of Man, or some such thing."

Swift Runner stared, mouth agape. Abruptly she sat down. Loud, uninhibited laughter erupted from her wide mouth. She practically hooted with glee. Tears of joy appeared in her eyes as the laughs diminished.

Joshua Donner stared in complete bafflement.

Fully recovered, Swift Runner explained that her Crow name was Man Killer. She went on to explain her warrior status and how sometimes she had strange powers. Because the Crow came to fear her, they decided that marrying her to Joshua was the perfect solution to their problem.

Flabbergasted, Joshua thought for a moment. He walked to where she sat beside the stream, smiled and held out his hand as though to help her up. He said, "It is too bad there were things said to make us think differently of each other."

Swift Runner took his hand, but instead of rising she pulled him down beside her. She looked into his eyes, returned his smile, and replied, "All those times you approached me ... they were because you thought my name was Man Lover? And that maybe I might want a man in my blanket?"

Joshua wasn't sure, but the way Swift Runner's eyes were twinkling, he thought she was laughing at him.

"Well, not every time. But ... most of the times," he said.

She threw her head back and laughed. Joshua tried

hard not to join her, but her laugh was infectious. To change the subject, he asked, "Why carry a bow with you to pick berries?"

The smile left her face and she looked deep into his eyes as though there the answer could be found to any questions she might have.

Still holding his gaze, she gestured across the stream toward the berry patch and said, "If I am over there and you are with our horses," she nodded in the direction of their stock, "how else would I be able to help you if you were attacked?"

Stunned by the obvious sincerity of her remark, Joshua was speechless. He didn't know what to say. Before he had a chance to speculate any further, she spoke the words that marked the real beginning of their relationship.

"You are my husband. While we are together your life is my life."

The touch on his knee was light. Feeling the warmth of the sun on his face, Joshua opened his eyes expecting to see Swift Runner's beautiful face. Instead, he stared into the brown eyes of Curly. The young Lakota looked away. The trapper's gaze was drawn to his right where the sun had broken through the clouds in the west.

"We must go, Joshua."

Curly's quiet words brought the trapper to his feet and to his senses. His toes tingled with the encroaching cold. Noticing that he still clutched the book, Joshua quickly stuffed the leather bound volume back into the rawhide parfleche. He felt a momentary panic as he asked, "How long did I sleep?"

Curly Hair handed him a piece of jerky to go with a fleeting smile and said, "Not long. I have been taught not to pamper my horses."

The Lakota turned away to gather his belongings and

to continue his watch of their back-trail.

Dazzled as much by the boy's small joke, as he was that he had actually slept, Josh stepped to the side. He couldn't get over it; Curly Hair made a joke. Joshua quickly relieved himself, made sure the cap was secure beneath his rifle's hammer, and made ready to leave. He noticed where the bark had been stripped from several aspen by foraging elk and wondered about their current whereabouts. Pushing the thought aside Joshua tugged at his clothing, brushed the icicles free of his moustache and beard, and adjusted the set of his revolver behind the broad belt. Already he was feeling the cold begin to work its way inside his heavy hunting shirt. He bit a piece off the jerky and in between chews beckoned to Curly, "Come, Warrior, this old war horse is getting impatient to run."

# ELEVEN

The Blackfoot scout, Weasel Fur, neared the base of the cliff. He was puzzled by the tracks he discovered in a sheltered portion of the trail. It was a spot where an overhang protected it from the heavy snowfall. Not only were there a set of pony tracks leading up the trail, there were now two sets moving away ahead of him. It looked like the pony stealer had help ... that someone had come to meet him. He grinned with anticipation at the newfound opportunity. To acquire two horses instead of just one made the warrior's heart beat at a much faster rate.

Although blind in one eye, the handicap didn't hinder him as much as he wanted others to think. The fact was that as a hunter and warrior, Weasel Fur was something of a failure. Lack of interest and misfortune were the prime causes of his downfall. With the pony stealer, he saw a situation that could quickly turn his medicine from bad to good. Dog Killer had given him the means to redeem himself. He was determined not to let the chance slip by. He lengthened his stride. At the bottom of the cliff the timber closed about him as though he had stepped into a large council lodge. Tall pine and skeletal aspen were in abundance everywhere. The pony tracks swept through the trees and entered a small clearing. Stepping into the meadow he stopped and listened. A crackling of underbrush came from his right. Certain that one of the horses had circled back, Weasel Fur rushed across the open to the edge of the dense trees opposite the spot where the noise was steadily increasing. The pony is running right into my waiting hands, he thought.

A startling snort and shrill whistle sent Weasel Fur's heart plummeting. Suddenly, snow flew in all directions as a gigantic bull elk burst into the open! Head up, antlers spread across its broad back, the terrified elk ran straight at Weasel Fur. A rolling, bulging eye glared while flaring nostrils expelled clouds of frost above a gaping, yellow tooth-filled mouth. This horrid image dominated the warrior's vision. Flying snow was everywhere and thrusting legs towered above him as he fell back in a futile struggle to get out of the way. In passing, a flaying hoof struck his leg a glancing blow. The brief pain only added to his misery as he lay in the snow and listened to the fading sounds of the running elk as it smashed through the underbrush. Struggling to his feet, Weasel Fur morosely limped forward and resumed following the pony trail.

Dog Killer stopped; his mittened hand briefly rubbed the scar tissue on his lips. Looking at the sky, he noticed that the snow was letting up. The two Blackfeet in single file behind him stopped also. The pipe-holder smiled grimly and thought, the Cold Maker has changed his mind. Perhaps he will let the sun shine on us this day. Using an abrupt hand sign the leader signaled his warriors to follow. With their snowshoes fastened to the back of their small packs, they moved along the trail swiftly but silently. All three pairs of eyes were constantly on the lookout for any unseen danger.

Shortly before coming off the cliff trail, Dog Killer saw the same tracks that Weasel Fur had discovered. His reading of the tracks, however, was different. Rather than backtrack to where his two warriors had left the trail, his instincts told him that they were now chasing two thieves, both on foot. Dog Killer increased their pace to a ground-eating trot. When the pine and other trees closed about them, they slowed their manner of movement and became more concerned with stealth rather than speed. Upon entering the small clearing they immediately saw where Weasel Fur had his confrontation with the *ponokau* (elk). After quickly reading the sign, the pipe-holder cursed when he saw that his warrior had followed the pony tracks rather than swing to the east to try to intercept the pony stealer. Dog Killer quickly checked the priming on his flint-lock musket. After his two remaining warriors had also seen to their weapons, he led them on an angle to the east where he hoped to seize his prey or at least to discover their tracks. The three lean figures moved through the trees with the grace of wolves. The condensation from their breath drifted behind them and rapidly dissipated in the frigid air. Their ghostly forms flitted between the snow-laden trees so quickly as to be nearly invisible.

# TWELVE

The storm was no more. Swift Runner was enjoying the new weather. The sun was shining but was slowly fading in the West. Thoughts of her husband lifted her eyes beyond the narrow ribbon of river to her front. The mountains thrust toward the bright blue sky with an air of defiance and strength that only Wakan Tanka could have created.

Her gaze was interrupted by the sudden flight of several birds from a clump of willows along the edge of the river. With her chin raised as though still watching the mountains, Swift Runner's eyes were carefully searching the top of the cut bank near the water's stony shore. Her right hand slipped inside her coat until it closed over the smooth, wooden handle of her revolver. There! To her left the ears and neck ruff of a gray wolf showed in profile through the brush above the cut bank. When she saw the dip in the ground just before cresting the top of the bank, she knew what to do. For just an instant she would be out of sight. Swift Runner slipped her left foot back until she was able to hook it behind the rawhide braid that encircled Sosa's flanks in front of his croup. Hissing the Lakota warning "A-ah" at a watching Heyoka, she pulled the pistol free of her coat and heel-tapped the Appaloosa down into the dry wash. As the small horse climbed up the other side, the woman twisted her left arm into the other braided sling, wrapped behind Sosa's withers and around the brisket, and dug in her heels.

The young Crow scout listened carefully. On the far side of the cut-bank, he heard the small horse's hooves scrabble for footing as it lunged up and over the bank. Sinew-notched arrow pulled to his ear, the crouching Crow glanced at the riderless horse as it plowed over the summit in a flurry of flying snow. He immediately lowered his bow, straightened, and looked back over the cut-bank. At that very instant a large wolf with bared fangs and braced forelegs appeared directly in front of him; yellow eyes that fastened onto his black ones froze him in his moccasins. The Crow warrior was not a seasoned one; his heart seemed to have magically leaped up and lodged in his throat.

At the same time that a low growl erupted from the snarling mouth, he heard a rasping, metallic click come from his rear. By that time, his surprise had been so complete that he lost his grip on his arrow, and he was all but defenseless. His only thought at the time was the foolish wish that the wolf did not show more anger because of the skin of his brother that he wore as a headdress. Swallowing loudly, the young Crow slowly turned. A beautiful Indian woman, who's moccasins proclaimed her as Lakota, had magically appeared on the back of the mountain pony and was pointing a pistol at him. Mouth suddenly dry as dust, he swallowed again.

Heyoka had given Swift Runner the time to swing back up onto Sosa's back and cock and aim her revolver at the young Crow. When the mountain horse leaped over the bank, Swift Runner was hanging on its offside where the Crow, with a quick glance, had not seen her. In Crow, she asked, "Where are those you scout for?"

In a shaky voice, he replied, "They are near the foot

of the mountain. We are searching for a raiding party of Blackfeet. It is believed they are of the Blood tribe. Two suns ago they raided our village and killed two old ones ... then stole ponies."

Regaining some of his lost courage, the youth asked, "How did you know that I was here?"

Swift Runner, holding her aim steady, answered, "Because wolves do not wear feathers."

The young warrior flushed with shame, knowing it was pure vanity that had him add a hawk's feather to his wolf headdress. He wondered at the purity of her handling of the Crow language. His eyes widened as the realization of who he was speaking to pierced his awareness.

"You are Man Killer?" he asked.

"No longer. I am now known as Swift Runner."

The young warrior stared. When he spoke, it was with great respect.

"I was still a small boy when you left our band. Your skill with the bow has become legend."

"What is your name, boy?"

"Pony Finder."

Nodding she asked, "Who leads your revenge party?"

The boy first hesitated and then replied, "He Who Rides Alone."

Swift Runner grinned. An impish light entered her eyes as she said, "Tell him I asked if he still sleeps alone. He will know why I ask."

The youth straightened as he asked, "You are letting me go?"

"Of course, I am not at war with the Crow. Tell He Who Rides Alone that if our paths cross I wish him no harm. I am only looking for my husband, who I fear is in danger."

Swift Runner lowered the hammer, and the trigger disappeared up into the pistol's frame. As she pushed the pistol behind her belt, the Crow stared in wonder at the strange gun; then he gaped as the legendary woman, Man Killer, spoke to the wolf in Lakota.

"Heyoka, *hopo* (Clown, let us go)."

As the wolf's leap carried him past Pony Finder, his heavy coat brushed his arm sending shivers of fear down his spine. He didn't move. He had been so enthralled with meeting the woman warrior that he had completely forgotten the wolf at his back. He shivered again as he recalled the large fangs dripping with menace and the penetrating yellow eyes.

Without another glance at the Crow youth, Swift Runner spun her pony and rode up river to the north. The wolf was a dark cloud floating alongside the loping mountain horse.

Still shaken, Pony Finder continued to watch her and the wolf until they became small like insects. He watched while they, having found a place to ford the river, crossed over and disappeared among the trees.

The western sky was ablaze with color as the Crow trotted toward his waiting pony. His lingering thought on the incident was how close he had come to death and of having to join his friends and ancestors beyond the stars.

# THIRTEEN

The one-eyed Blackfoot, Weasel Fur, stopped tracking and slipped to the side of the trail. He peered out from behind a snow-covered bush at the tops of several pine and white birch. Carefully keeping himself hidden, he moved closer until he was able to see the pony tracks leading into the trees. The small grove of trees was located in a low area at the base of the incline. Weasel Fur was out of sight near the top of the hill. As far as he could see, the horses' tracks led right in among the trees. He felt a tingle of excitement begin to grow in his belly. He wanted those two ponies very much. After being humiliated by the *ponokau* (elk), the unlucky Blackfoot had a desperate need to redeem himself. Quietly he waited to see if the horses were still in the grove of trees. From where he crouched he could see no tracks leaving the grove. He checked the wind to be certain his scent was not blowing in their direction and settled down to wait.

Weasel Fur could not wait any longer. He glanced at the color showing in the western sky and knew his time was running out. With the wind safely caressing his face, he began his approach. The shadows from trees and bushes were growing long as the day's end grew near and Weasel

Fur used them to his best advantage. By the time he reached the edge of the trees, he was very pleased with himself. It wasn't until he had entered the woods, spied the horses, and felt the icy muzzle of a musket barrel press against his cheek that he realized his mistake.

Later he would ask himself: why would the horses have stayed inside the trees? Had they been free they would have roamed to the nearby prairie where grasses were more abundant.

When the explosion did not happen, Weasel Fur slowly turned his head and looked into the laughing eyes of Iron Heart, a Blood warrior from a neighboring tribe. Upon recognition of a Blackfeet ally, relief washed over him with the cleansing effect of a bath in a winter stream. To Weasel Fur it was like greeting someone from his village.

Not only were the Bloods close geographically to their allies, the Blackfeet (Piegan), they were so similar in other ways most mountain men considered them to be just another tribe of Blackfeet.

The lower half of Iron Heart's face had been painted by dipping his hand in red paint and placing it over his mouth, symbolizing the drinking of his enemy's blood.

All thought was swept from the one-eyed warrior's mind except the gratification that comes with knowing that he was alive and with friendly warriors. It wasn't until then that he noticed the other horses spread throughout the birch and pine. Off to one side a heavily armed warrior held the rawhide leads to a pair of horses that weren't painted.

Derisive laughter gurgled from the garishly painted mouth of Iron Heart thus encouraging other shadowy figures to leave their places of concealment and step into the open.

Iron Heart's gravel voice said, "Who would think that, while waiting for the Cold Maker to stop the snow, we would find such fine horses for the taking so close to home?" He paused and faced his audience. "Also, this fine Piegan scalp," he joked.

Appreciative laughter rumbled from the shadows.

With the realization that his quest for horses and glory was at an end, Weasel Fur's hope plummeted. The taste of defeat was bitter and the added mockery lit a fire of rage inside his heart.

No one had ever questioned the one-eyed warrior's courage, just his judgment and lack of ambition. Therefore, when his fury burst from his mouth no one made an attempt to deride or ridicule.

"Who leads you? Who among you is the pipe-holder?" The one-eyed Piegan's voice cracked with the sharp sound of a tree splitting from the cold.

Iron Heart stepped forward and thumped a fist against his chest as he proclaimed, "I am the pipe-holder, Piegan. We have come from the Crow with horses and scalps!" His boast brought murmurs of agreement from the handful of warriors. "Why are you here? Where are the owners of those horses?" As he spoke, Iron Heart jabbed a finger at Weasel Fur and gestured toward the unpainted pair of ponies standing nearby.

Refusing to be intimidated and not wishing to reveal his ignorance concerning the last question, Weasel Fur heatedly replied, "I am here in pursuit of a Cut-throat pony stealer who had stolen the war horse from the great warrior, Dog Killer. The war horse has returned, yet Dog Killer still wants to remove the Cut-throat's liver."

Voices muttered approval, wanting him to continue.

"As is his right as pipe-holder on this revenge raid, he told me to follow the horses' trail. As you can see, the Cut-throat Sioux is not with his horses; he must now be on foot. His two horses must be returned to our village."

Iron Heart slowly nodded his head and gestured at one of his warriors who then isolated the two horses.

Several of the Blood warriors moved in closer. As he

spoke, Weasel Fur watched closely hoping his words would have the desired effect.

"Do you wish for more blood? It could easily be had. Somewhere between here and our mountain villages the Cut-throats run free ... in Piegan and Blood country!"

Anger began to rear its ugly head and sweep through the listening warriors. Blackfeet hated trespassers on their land, no matter which tribe.

Becoming carried away by his own oratory, the one-eyed Piegan paused. Once again he saw the opportunity for plunder. Perhaps, he thought, the Cut-throat has one of the Big Knife's (white man's) guns. Greed overcame his normal indifference, as he added, "Give me the loan of a horse and I will show where we should find this Cut-throat pony stealer."

# FOURTEEN

With the sky creating a pale gold backdrop, the white-tail deer burst from the clump of aspen in a shower of flying snow. Joshua was so startled he stumbled and nearly fell. Excited, Curly Hair shouted encouragement to the fleeing buck as it flagged its white tail and lunged through the drifted snow. With his antlers and dark body stark against a white winter background, the white-tail was a sight to behold. It was a picture that captured Joshua's heart with its beauty. Neck arched, head erect, the deer ran and leaped with great speed and agility. In his excitement, Curly gripped Joshua's shoulder in a comrade-like fashion. Two more jumps and the deer was gone, as was Curly's hand.

Joshua quickly regained his stride and tried to slow his breathing so he wouldn't be sucking in huge draughts of icy air. While he ran, Curly twisted and turned to study the surrounding terrain. The movement broke Joshua's rhythm, but he knew that it was necessary for them to keep a constant lookout. The leader of the Blackfeet had already split his war party once and the trapper knew there was no rule saying he couldn't do it again. Joshua was painfully aware that they could be attacked from any direction at any moment.

They were nearing the base of the mountain and were into the gentle swells of the foothills. Occasional rock abutments and pinnacles dotted the landscape; even caves and bunches of lowland birch trees and juniper were joining the towering pine and stately aspen.

Joshua slowed his pace and tried to think in spite of his headache. He was undecided which way to go. Before he made any major commitment he needed to know the whereabouts of the Blackfeet. As he speculated, Joshua started his run across a rocky area. A gap over a rocky draw was bridged by several solid appearing dead trees that nature had placed there. Without any hesitation, he started across the natural snow-covered bridge, picking the larger of the deadfalls. Halfway across there was a loud crunch and Joshua felt the tree give way beneath his moccasined feet. Before he could recover his balance, the dead tree collapsed. Releasing Curly's legs Joshua shoved him into the clear and attempted to follow. It was close but he didn't quite avoid the falling, splintered mass of tree trunk and broken limbs. He landed hard; his head and back took the bulk of the impact. Curly Hair's medicine was good. He landed on the cushioning branches of a young juniper and rolled clear.

Momentarily dazed, Joshua's ears echoed with the crackling of shattered branches. As his head cleared, he put his hand down to push himself up and his arm broke through the lattice of broken tree limbs and branches. Joshua didn't move. To his growing horror, he felt fur ... a moving mass of fur!

With a roar that took Joshua's breath away, a huge grizzly rose from the pile of broken branches and logs and stood on his hind legs, towering nearly ten feet tall. Tree trunks were dislodged and cast aside like scattered kindling. Fortunately, Joshua was on one of the logs that was knocked out of the way. He landed in the snow near a wide-eyed Curly Hair. The young Lakota was trying unsuccessfully to notch an arrow onto a taut, twisted sinew bowstring and watch the grizzly at the same time. The bear roared again, his breath a rising cloud of white. Joshua and Curly Hair involuntarily covered their ears from the onslaught of noise. Slobber flew from curled lips and dripped from the long, yellow fangs. Joshua was struggling desperately to disentangle himself from the refuse.

Without taking his eyes off the giant bear, Curly Hair scrambled to his feet. Trying to avoid putting his full weight on his injured leg, he clutched at Joshua's arm and helped him up. The big trapper, pale eyes locked on the roaring, enraged grizzly, grabbed his Hawken from the snow and practically threw the Lakota boy onto his back. Stumbling in his attempt to hurry, Joshua ran down the littered gully.

From his higher viewing point Curly Hair glanced behind them and gave a quick thanks to Wakan Tanka. The mato (bear) was not pursuing! He felt the coil and shift of the wasichu's muscles as he spun clear of the debris in the gully and ran downhill following the natural curve of the snow-covered draw. The loud, terrifying roars diminished, then stopped. Looking back, the young Lakota was in time to see the bear drop back to all fours and disappear from sight inside his tangled den. While relief quieted his thudding heart, Curly Hair's head spun with an unanswered question. Why, when Joshua began to fall, did he take the time to throw me clear? I do not understand, he thought. His worry and wonder soon drifted away as the jarring rhythm of Joshua's stride made him more conscious of more immediate problems. With eyes narrowed against the sun's fading glare, the Sioux boy's gaze swept everywhere watching for more danger. He welcomed the sight of the country opening before them as they neared the plain. His thinking had barely returned to the enigma of the white man, when Joshua's breathing began to labor and he shifted resetting Curly Hair's weight. It was a sure sign that fatigue was setting in. As the sun died in the west their shadows lengthened; the cold intensified and increased the condensation emitting from their mouths with each breath. Both changes made them more visible to the searching eye. Perhaps that was why the Blackfeet spied them first.

"*Hii, yii, yii, yi, yi!*"

The dreaded war cry coming from their right front caused Joshua to stumble and Curly Hair to gape in surprise and fear. A party of mounted warriors rode into sight and swerved toward them.

Joshua saw right away they were Blood Blackfeet, neighbors and allies of the Piegan.

The driving hooves of their ponies were sending clumps of snow in all directions as they struggled to run through the drifted snow. Before Curly Hair could think what to do, Joshua stopped, spun around and began to run back up the same draw.

Taking a firmer grip on Curly's legs, he left the draw and ran parallel to its twisted length and deliberately sought out trees and brush, making it harder for the Indian ponies to climb the slippery slope. The Blood warriors, howling like banshees from hell, had a different idea. They left their trail and swept up the same draw Joshua and Curly had left. The easier riding was helping them to draw closer with each thrusting lunge of their horses' hooves. Joshua's breath was coming in great whoops as he strove to drive himself harder. The Blood Blackfeet were almost parallel when suddenly Joshua swerved to the right.

With horrified eyes tearing from the cold, Curly Hair saw that they were going to cross directly in front of the blood-thirsty warriors. At that very instant, it became startlingly clear that with their angle of ascent they were going to pass over the clogged draw just above the grizzly's den.

"Is your bow ready?"

Joshua's Lakota came to Curly Hair's ears in gasps and heaves. Pulling an arrow free, he replied with a trembling voice, "Yes, Joshua." Pausing he then asked, "Is this where we make our stand and die?"

"We are not the ones who will die!" Joshua breathlessly shouted.

They began to cross above the clogged draw when Joshua deliberately collapsed into the snow. Curly rolled free, a notched arrow ready on his bow.

The howling pack of warriors was closing fast when Joshua shouted, "Shoot down into the bear's den!"

Curly hesitated.

"Do it! And keep shooting as fast as you can!"

Curly Hair pulled his bowstring taut until the arrow's fletching tickled his cheek. He released. The shaft was a flicker of light before disappearing inside the pile of timber. A savage growl reverberated from the wood-filled depths.

A pair of young Blackfeet, faces streaked with vermilion, were leading the pack and were closing rapidly. Choosing to deal with the more immediate danger, the young Sioux quickly loosed a shaft that struck the lead rider high in the stomach. Grimacing with pain, he slid from his pony and into the snow at the base of the dead trees.

Suddenly, the slope echoed with the boom of a Blackfoot's musket. The ball whistled harmlessly by Curly's head.

Joshua angrily shouted something in English, then pulled his revolver free and shot down into a space between two battered logs. The pistol's flat report was still ringing when a horrific roar assailed their ears.

With remarkable speed, the enraged grizzly charged out of its wood and rock den on all fours, sending pieces of splintered wood flying in all directions. The leading Blackfeet tried desperately to stop their ponies. Because of the snow the horses slid and fell in their attempts to get clear of the frenzied monster as it closed with them. Then he was in among them! Screams from both horse and man rent the winter air. Frost rose in ever increasing clouds as the grizzly ripped and tore through the scattered, terrified warriors and fallen horses. Blood colored the snow everywhere as the bear stood on his hind legs and using both front legs, raked and slapped, ripped and tore.

Curly watched in horror as the grizzly's bloody jaws closed over one Blackfoot's head and ripped him open from throat to belly with one sweep of his claws. Tossing him aside, the bear roared and again dropped to all fours. With the speed of a wolf, the grizzly raced across the bloodied draw and caught a pony and rider from behind just as they were about to get clear.

Something clutched his arm! Curly Hair's heart seemed to stop beating. Joshua, his face twisted with pain, or regret, had a powerful grip on his arm.

"We must go ... now!" Joshua's voice cracked with authority.

Curly quickly climbed onto his back. Joshua, rifle in one hand, pistol in the other, ran with a newly found strength. Suddenly, a garishly painted face beneath a fur hat, with a blanket billowing out behind him, lunged toward him from a clump of aspen. Without breaking stride Joshua let go of Curly's right leg and fired his Paterson pistol directly into the middle of the painted, hate-filled face. There was an orange flash and a loud, flat report; then a gout of smoke, and the Blackfoot, braids wildly flying, collapsed backwards into the snow.

Joshua ran on.

Quickly, the sound of the fight diminished until only an occasional roar or scream reached them. Darkness was closing fast and their need to get as far away as possible was of the utmost importance. Trying not to slip, Joshua lengthened his strides. He was thinking of the gunshots. He had tried to avoid the noise by having Curly roust the bear out with his arrows, but as soon as the musket was fired he figured he might as well let her rip. Those who were chasing them on foot, he thought, will hear one shot just as quick as a handful.

He ran on.

While he ran he tried not to think of the possibility of Blood and Piegan warriors closing in from all sides. Whenever the boy moved, Joshua felt it. And he knew from the constant movement that Curly was doing his job and keeping a close lookout behind and on their sides. The direct front was his own responsibility. Consequently, he tried to keep his mind blank yet ready for whatever would occur, but it was hopeless. Joshua's conscience was bothering him. His mind kept filling with pictures of the dead and the dying: of the grizzly, using his rage as a weapon to drive the intruders from his domain, and the poor slaughtered horses, wanting nothing but to please their owners and have food and shelter. He even found pity for a few of the Blackfeet; some were only boys playing at war.

He ran on.

With quivering legs and faltering strides, Joshua made his own trace through the sparkling virgin snow. The fading light had turned the blanketing white powder to orange and then red, shifting to purple. In spite of the darkness that was slowly settling over them like a giant buffalo hide, he continued to concentrate on the simple chore of placing one foot after the other into the exhausting snow. Soon all that could be heard was the repetition of the trapper's steady footfalls and the rasp of his breathing as he fled the horror and ran for both of their lives.

# FIFTEEN

The mountains were a darker mass that loomed high above, dominating the shortened horizon. Swift Runner had made a small fire that could only be seen from a few feet away. Heyoka had left for a while. Upon his return to the fire, a detected tuft of rabbit fur stuck to his muzzle brought a tiny smile to her lips. She was pleased that he remained independent, yet still chose to be with her. Crouched among some willows near a narrow stream, the Lakota woman relaxed and tried to shake the worry that had become so much a part of her day. She listened to the sounds Sosa made as she grazed nearby, and she thought of Joshua.

Earlier, as Wi was completing his journey and the Sky Father was painting the western horizon with colors of gold and orange, Swift Runner had been setting up camp. Unexpectedly she had sensed something stir inside her head. There was a jolt followed by a glimmer of instant awareness. A blurred picture with vivid color and lurid sound flashed through her mind. Her brief, interrupted vision was so real she staggered and dropped the parfleche she had removed from her pony's back. Joshua was running! In her mind, she heard cries of pain and screams of rage. He ran as though burdened with some great weight. There was an explosion of fire and smoke as a hazy figure was flung backwards into the

91

snow. Joshua ran on through the snow and trees.

The vision had been so convincing, Swift Runner's fear for her husband escalated to the point where she had packed up her goods, saddled Sosa, and rode on until darkness and chill had forced her to stop near the small stream.

Knowing there would be a moon that night, she flipped the hood of her capote up and settled down to wait. She pulled the hood close around her face so that the warmth of her breath would comfort her. Once the moon was up, she thought, they would ride on. To keep the lingering fear away, Swift Runner tried to relax and thought of happier, warmer days. She smiled as she remembered a warm night during the Moon When The Ponies Shed.

They lay side by side on a blanket watching the wonder of the stars spread out above them. A gentle breeze cooled their damp bodies with fingers gloved in satin. After making love neither felt the need for words. Each found fulfillment and pleasure with simply being together.

They were camped near the Musselshell River, east of the Crazy Mountains. For several days they had thought they were being followed by a pair of Pawnee they had met further south. At the time of the meeting there had been distance between them, and the Pawnee had quietly watched them from afar. They were too far away to tell if they were painted. Joshua had decided the best thing to do would be to ignore them, so they had gone on their way. The following day, while crossing a flat stretch of prairie, Swift Runner (who was still known as Man Killer) caught a fleeting glimpse of two distant figures disappearing behind a small, lightly wooded hill. She and Joshua waited patiently, but the riders never showed themselves. In time they dismissed them as having been a couple of mustangs or antelope on the roam and rode on. Both she and Joshua had decided that the

Pawnee were a long way north of home, and if they were following, looking for plunder and scalps, they would soon give it up and move south.

The following day they had indeed seen riders but never saw enough of them to determine if they were the Pawnee. They rode hard the remainder of the day and well into the night before camping. Both were certain that if they were being followed they had lost them. At sunup they rode north through the gradually greening prairie and established their camp beside the Musselshell. The remainder of the day they spent in camp, cleaning their gear, finding graze for their stock, and making love in the afternoon's waning light.

At Joshua's touch, she looked into his blue eyes, dark because of the shade from a tall cottonwood, and wondered at his gentleness. She had never been happier. The lonely years among the Crow seemed another lifetime ago. Her husband gave so much and asked so little in return; it did not seem right. She knew very little about wasichus; all those she had seen were full of boasting, bad manners, and selfish thought. This one was unlike any other. Joshua's soft voice interrupted her thoughts.

"What are you thinking, oh mighty Man Killer?"

Hearing the tease in his voice, she laughed. But for the first time in her young life, she was ashamed of her Crow name.

"I am thinking that I shall take another name."

Joshua looked embarrassed.

"Wonumayin (A mistake has been made). I meant no disrespect."

"I know that is true, Joshua. I just feel that my name no longer suits me." She pulled him close and nuzzled the hollow beneath his ear. "Perhaps you were right and I should be called, Woman Who Loves Man, or Man Lover."

Joshua laughed and rolled over on top of her. She pushed him away and with a girlish giggle jumped to her feet. She stood still for a moment and let the breeze caress her naked body as she looked down on him. Except for his face and hands, Joshua's body was as white as the bark on the talking trees the whites call aspen. His golden hair and beard reminded her of their leaves just before the winter gods blow them from the tree.

Joshua beckoned with his arms, as he said, "Come to me, oh lover of man." He grinned and made a grab for her wrist.

Avoiding his hands, she replied, "If I do not leave now my new name may become, She Who Relieves Herself on Blankets."

His laughter followed her as she skipped down the small incline toward the river. Moving into the bushes, she quickly relieved herself and turned toward their camp. Wi's fading light shining on the river winked at her, catching her eye. Unable to resist she ran the extra distance to the river and waded in, ignoring the shocking cold.. She splashed the frigid water up onto her arms and legs and sat down, letting the soothing, icy tingle wash over her. Glancing toward where Joshua was lying, she felt her stomach knot. He was not there!

With a concentrated effort she calmed herself and the tension abruptly left her. He probably had the same need that she had had, she reasoned, and had stepped into the bushes. She glanced up river and the knot came back with a vengeance. Her stomach felt bruised. Less than an arrow's flight away, on her side of the river, a painted Pawnee was sitting his horse quietly watching her.

She knew immediately he was Pawnee by the hair style and war paint.

On the plains, the shaved head with a narrow roach of hair down the middle was almost as certain a means of identifying the hated tribe as their language.

With a quick glance to the camp and back at the

Pawnee, she gauged her chances. It would be close, but she thought she could reach her weapons before he rode her down. She stood up. The water caused her body to glisten in the yellow light. Not looking directly at him, she slowly waded through the thigh deep river water to shore.

The scream of a mountain cat pierced the night and sent the Lakota woman's eyes darting to her right. He was still there! A loud splash swiveled her gaze to the opposite shore. Another Pawnee had galloped his horse noisily into the river and screamed his war cry. He slapped his pony across the rump and screamed again as he urged his war horse into a faster, lunging stride.

Head down, she ran for her life! Her side vision picked up the first Pawnee as he also kicked his pony into a gallop. The splashing noises ceased as the other Indian's horse left the water. The thunder of horses' hooves encouraged her to run like she never had before. Arms pumping, legs driving, she fairly flew across the flat ground and raced up the gradual incline toward their camp. She looked up. Her heart swelled as hope surged through her body. Joshua, naked as the day he was born, was standing near some cottonwoods at the far side of their campsite. Wildflowers fell unnoticed from his hand as he lunged into camp, grabbed his Hawken, aimed and fired.

The rifle ball buzzed over her head like an enraged hornet. Over the thunder of closing hooves, she heard the heavy ball hit. The ensuing scream that followed came from a disturbingly short distance away.

Not having time to reload, Joshua's eyes locked onto the remaining hard-riding Pawnee. He ran toward him and reversed his plains rifle to use as a club. Man Killer blew past him like a whirlwind.

He stepped forward to meet the oncoming warrior. The Pawnee was so close, Joshua could see the sweat glistening on his painted face and shaved head. Beneath his

95

hate-filled countenance, a necklace of human finger-bones bounced on his naked chest. A startling sound, like the rapid wings of a grouse, whipped past his ear.

The Pawnee, war club poised, gasped as the arrow pierced his chest. Reflex caused him to rein in his pony as dark blood spilled over his pugnacious chin. Another shaft landed within an inch of the first, toppling him from the horse's back as lifeless as a sack of turnips. The Pawnee war horse shied away, trampling his dead master's body as he trotted off with a snort and toss of his head.

Joshua, stunned by the sudden turn of events, turned and looked at his wife. What a woman, he thought.

She stood perfectly still; only her eyes shifted as they searched the nearby terrain for movement. Completely naked, river water still beaded and streaked her moist, tawny-skinned body. Her left hand clutched her sinew-backed, horn bow; her right hand held a third arrow notched and ready to let fly. She must have felt Joshua's eyes. Still looking away, she grinned. Not until then did she turn and look at him. Joshua returned her smile and asked, "How does the name, Swift Runner, suit you?"

# SIXTEEN

A sharp pain lanced across the jagged wound on his forehead. Joshua opened his eyes to a black and blue world. The moon was up. Its eerie light changed the snowy terrain from white to light blue and everything else into shades of black or gray. He was shocked by how well he could see. A momentary dizziness gave birth to a pang of anxiety that brought him shakily to his feet. His hand found a sturdy birch that gave support until the dizziness passed. In mere seconds, Joshua was himself again.

Suddenly, he felt apprehensive and slowly turned in a circle looking the area over. To his right front he saw a slim, dark form that materialized into Curly Hair; his welcoming smile was a bright beacon on his dark, moon-tinted face.

"Did you rest well, Joshua?"

"I am rested, Curly. But you need sleep, also."

"I will have plenty of time for that when I return to my family. I think we must leave here."

Joshua looked around at their bleak surroundings. He remembered that they had climbed nearly halfway up the slope of the mountain before he had collapsed from sheer exhaustion. They were in a thicket of juniper, birch, and tall pine that, because of the bright moon, was full of deep shadows. It was fortunate, he thought, that earlier his body chose to fail him at this spot. The timbered grove just happened to have a good view of open ground in nearly every direction. Knowing that their Blackfeet pursuers would be able to see at least as well, he worried that their knowledge of the country would allow them to move more quickly in the moonlight. Nobody was going to sneak up on them, but on the other hand, they had to leave across the same open ground.

"You are right, my friend." With his words, he saw Curly glance his way with a puzzled expression, then quickly look away. Ignoring the look, Joshua smiled and asked, "Do you never feed your horses, Warrior?"

Curly's dazed expression left his face, and he laughed aloud as he dug a large piece of smoked meat free from Joshua's parfleche and handed it to him.

"Enjoy this, Tashunke (Horse)," Curly said, "Later I will find you some sweet grass."

While he finished munching jerky, Joshua chuckled to himself. Later, he scooped handfuls of clean snow into his mouth, savoring the cold moisture. Afterward, he gingerly rubbed the icy snow over his throbbing head wound and pulled some cloth remnants from his rawhide bag and made a clean bandage. Wanting to help, Curly tied leather strips around his head that held the bandage in place against his painful wound. While still keeping a close eye on the land, they swiftly gathered their 'possibles.' After painstakingly taking the Paterson apart, he reloaded his pistol and put it back together again. After Joshua checked to be sure the percussion cap was well seated on his rifle, they were ready to leave. As the boy limped over to pick up his rawhide parfleche, Joshua caught his eye. Curly Hair stopped and straightened as he asked, "What is wrong?"

Joshua's eyes lifted until he was looking north toward where the dark mass of the mountain met the lighter moonlit sky. He turned and faced the young Lakota and answered, "I know the Blackfeet are used to raiding in moonlight, so they will probably be hunting us right now. I do not know how well they track in this light, so I think the last thing they would expect would be for us to go higher. It means moving deeper into Blackfeet country instead of making a run for the plains."

Joshua shrugged, looked at Curly, and added, "Before we make any move, I want to know what your thoughts are on this."

Curly Hair was thoughtful for a moment. He met Joshua's gaze and swiftly replied, "I think you are right, Joshua. We must climb higher. Somehow, we need to find out how many Blackfeet are hunting us."

Joshua nodded, picked up his rifle and made ready to go. Facing Curly, he said, "When I sicked that bear on them Blackfeet, I had hoped to catch us a real horse."

He shook his head in frustration as he remembered how the Blackfeet had turned tail and run like a bunch of Digger Indians. With their fierce reputation as warriors and hunters, running was the last thing Joshua expected them to do.

"I never thought they would run," he added.

Curly Hair slipped the rawhide bag over his head and adjusted his bow and arrows. He glanced Joshua's way as he quietly informed him, "It was not your fault, Joshua. My grandfather told me that the Blackfeet feel that bears have special powers. It is perhaps the only thing they fear. They will not eat bear meat; they will not wear their furs. The few pelts that do come into their possession are given to their gods as offerings."

"I'll be damned," Joshua muttered in English. Turning his broad back, he bent over and placed his hands on his knees. In Lakota, he said, "Looks like you are stuck with the same old war horse. Let us hope this one does not get wind broke, or turn up lame."

# SEVENTEEN

The three raiders moved swiftly along the moonlight covered slope. Although ungainly, the snow-shoes were a necessity and the Blackfeet were still able to move with surprising speed through the new snow. As the snow's depth diminished so did the warriors' need for the clumsy foot equipment. Dog Killer and his two warriors stopped and removed their snowshoes. While tying his pair to the small pack on his back, the pipe-holder thought of earlier just before darkness when they had heard the distant gunfire.

He remembered being confused by the shooting, knowing that only one of the two warriors he had sent down the side of the cliff had a firearm. The gun noise had come from two different guns; neither sounded like the type of musket his warrior carried. Dog Killer instinctively felt that it was too far away for Weasel Fur to be involved. He recalled thinking that the fool was probably far out on the prairie chasing the two ghost ponies in the dark. The pipe-holder felt the shape of his horse talisman nestled in its pouch and prayed to *Napi* that his war medicine would aid him in his search for revenge.

Shortly after the popping of the guns it had become very dark and the three were forced to stop. They retreated into a heavy growth of pine for shelter and huddled in their blankets as they waited for Night Light to appear. They had waited until Night Light was showing all of herself before striking out on the trail once again.

The pipe-holder stood up and allowed his thoughts to return to the present as he signaled his men to take the trail. Released from the constriction of the snowshoes, the three ran at a trot through the blue moonlight. Dog Killer led them. While his eyes missed nothing, his mind continued to be saturated with thoughts of revenge. Already, he thought, this accursed Cut-throat has cost me much time and effort. I will find him and his accomplice and remove their feet and hands with my knife; their livers will be next followed by their hearts, if they have any. He ran on, driven by his blood-thirsty need. Dog Killer stopped. All thoughts of revenge flew away as an unexpected sight caught his eye.

Far ahead and down the slope, a pinpoint of light winked and flickered. The unexpected sight created confusion in the mind of the pipe-holder. He stared in disbelief at the flicker of a man-made fire. Only a fool, he thought, or a Blackfoot would dare build a fire this close to the land of the Blackfeet. He motioned his warriors forward and they moved toward the distant light that looked like a fallen star.

Not long after Night Light appeared, Weasel Fur stopped poking at his small fire and looked around him at the remains of Iron Heart's war party. Only four warriors and himself were left after the *omach-ku-kyaio* (grizzly), the Cut-throat, and Big Knife trapper had attacked them. Three men and two horses were killed. Whenever he thought of the grizzly, his heart felt like it was being squeezed. He and Iron Heart had escaped the bear's fury by reining their ponies out of the gully and into some trees on the east side of the draw. Iron Heart, eager to count coup, had left him and raced up the slope, vanishing into another clump of trees. Having enough excitement for one day, Weasel Fur's instinct for self-preservation kept him from joining the Blood warrior. Instead, he kept a close eye on the bear that was handily slaughtering his comrades only a long tomahawk throw away. In spite of his fear of the sacred bear, his attention was strangely drawn to where the Cut-throat and Big Knife crouched. With hate-filled eyes, he watched Big Knife with the Sioux on his back run to the right. He had seen right away how the trapper was running almost straight at Iron Heart. He felt a pang of envy, realizing that his Blood friend was about to count coup and acquire a pair of scalps and the Big Knife's rifle and pistol. The envy disappeared as quickly as the smoke and fire that erupted from the trapper's gun. He saw Iron Heart, arms flung wide, fall backwards down the slope where he sprawled in the snow as lifeless as a child's doll.

As his thoughts returned to the flickering shadows of the present, Weasel Fur added another stick of wood to their fire. He looked up at the remains of the raiding party and silently cursed. Of the four remaining warriors, only one was injured.

Tall Bird, a fierce warrior who had many coups, sat morosely nearby. He brooded and absently stroked his war medicine, a stuffed male cardinal that was tied to his right braid. Its redness added a cheerful dab of color to the somber scene. Earlier, when the bear attacked them, Tall Bird had broken his arm when his horse stepped into a hole hidden by the snow and spilled him onto some rocks. His pony's leg had broken in the fall. Tall Bird had quickly run away. His horse was later killed by the grizzly. The blood warrior was not happy. By leaving his pony, he felt that he had behaved badly. A veteran warrior, he sat and glared into the night, pointedly protecting his night vision by not looking at the fire. He cradled his arm, stroked his war medicine, and thought private thoughts of redemption.

Weasel Fur, his hopes of glory slowly drifting away, probed the coals of his fire with a green stick as if the answer to his problems could be found within the bed of glowing embers.

Tall Bird abruptly stood up and stared up toward the slope of the mountain. Weasel Fur got up and stared also. He couldn't see a thing except a rosy glow. He was so busy feeling sorry for himself, he had negligently stared into the fire. He looked at Tall Bird as he whispered, "What is wrong?"

"Someone comes," he explained.

Tall Bird hissed a command. The remaining warriors scooped up their weapons and disappeared among the trees.

Then Weasel Fur heard them also. Tiny sounds came to him from the night, familiar noises that brought with them memories of many winter raids. The measured steps and faint squeak of moccasins moving through snow sent waves of apprehension up his spine. "Dog Killer," he murmured under his breath.

# EIGHTEEN

Swift Runner rode Sosa through the encompassing world of blue snow and dark shadows. The moonlight was especially bright, showing her the way and aiding her in her search. Heyoka was a blurred shadow running alongside the mountain horse, gracefully dodging objects or floating over them like a dark cloud.

When the moon had first risen, she had pointed the horse in a straight line toward the dark mass of mountains where she knew Joshua ran for his life. Her extra-sensory instincts had pointed her toward a specific point and she had never deviated from it. When a tiny, fluttering light appeared near the base of the towering heights she was not surprised, only relieved that the spark of the fire was there and indicated human life. As she drew near she slowed Sosa to a walk; something did not feel right. There was a slight whisper in the wind. She knew immediately that her husband was not a part of the small fire at the base of the slope. She listened carefully to the sibilant wind. Ahead of her she was startled to see the ghost-like images of several horses slowly walking toward the fire. Her mountain pony drifted toward the ponies that were strangely converging toward the flickering fire. It is almost as though they are being led, she thought. At that instant, a web of clouds left the face of the moon and her view of the horses clarified. She suffered an emotional blow to her stomach when she realized that Indians were lying flat across their ponies' backs so as not to be seen. Swift Runner softly hissed the Lakota warning "A-ah." Heyoka melted into the shadows but stayed close.

Knowing the grave danger she was in, she instinctively slid back so that she was lying flat on Sosa's spotted back, exactly like the quiet warriors to her front. Two arrows and her horn bow were clutched in her left hand. Once again she slipped her left foot into the braided rawhide sling that encircled her pony's flanks in front of the croup. Carefully, her skin tingling with excitement, she guided Sosa toward the right side of the group of horses. She wanted to be on the outside of the war party so that she had all the warriors on her left side. As the Appaloosa closed with the slowly advancing war party, Swift Runner quickly found and grasped the loop braided into her pony's mane.

The loop in his mane and the rawhide sling around Sosa's body would enable her to hang on the off-side of his body and shoot arrows from beneath his neck.

A soft nicker from one of the horses, which was instantly cut off by a strong red hand, caused her heart to leap toward her throat. Her own hand had reflexively grabbed Sosa's muzzle before a reply could be blown through the quivering nostrils. Up ahead she saw that the moving horses were mingling in with other horses. Her gaze swept toward the winking fire and saw more Indians. Siha Sappa (Blackfeet)! She recognized them from their heavy braids and winter dress. They were having some kind of discussion. She thanked Wakan Tanka for not making Joshua a prisoner among them. Only a few Blackfeet were mounted and there were not any pony herd guards.

It looked as though she was soon to be caught up in a fight that was none of her business. A fighting rage directed toward this unexpected obstacle moved through her body as she mentally prepared to make battle.

One of the warriors raised his head for a peek at the enemy fire. In profile, she saw the stiffened hair rising from his sloping forehead and aquiline nose. Looking closer she saw the vermilion part above the temple along with the small braid in front of the loose flowing hair. Crow! Her mind raced ... Pony Finder's revenge raiders! Confused by an unexpected loyalty she did not know she had, Swift Runner did not know what to do. She had apparently lived with the Crow too long to be able to kill without being provoked. Before she was able to decide her next move, her decision was made for her by the Crow.

"*Hooo-Kii-Hi*!" The Crow war cry split the night into fragments. For less time than two heartbeats, Blackfeet faces turned their way and stared. Several more Crow war cries rent the quiet night with blood-curdling intensity! Blackfeet scattered in every direction. Those on horseback bravely spun their mounts and galloped to meet the enemy. The Blackfeet war cry joined the Crows' and the night became a din of hideous noise. Crow heels pounded pony flanks and the whole war party surged forward waving their weapons. A rifle exploded with a thunderous, "Crack!"

The boom of an occasional musket added to the night noise. Throwing caution to the night winds, Swift Runner straightened and swung her mountain pony to the right, away from the hard-riding Crow. She threw a last glance toward the fighting and saw four figures, dark against the moonlit snow, break away and run northeast up the slope. Puzzled by their actions, she kept her eye on the four men angling single file up the mountain slope. A new clamor from the fight spooked Sosa, and he began to spin in an erratic circle. Swift Runner hung on and jerked on the rawhide rein. As she brought him under control her eyes did not leave the fleeing Blackfeet. She knew they were not Crow because they were on foot and were running toward the heart of Blackfeet country. Her instincts told her that they were not merely running away from a fight, but that whoever led them had another reason. And the only reason Swift Runner could think of that would draw a Blackfoot away from a bloodletting would be the prospect of spilling more blood. Suddenly, her vision blanched and she reeled, nearly losing hold of the reins. Grasping her pony's mane she saw in her mind's eye a flash of Joshua standing, silhouetted against the skyline of a ridge. Incredulous, she saw what appeared to be an Indian perched on his back.

"Boom!" Another gunshot ripped through the night. The musket ball buzzed by her ear and broke the image of her vision. Abruptly, Swift Runner was again aware of the screams of the dying and the whoops and shouts of the triumphant. The vision had left her momentarily weak and sick; it was all she could do to stay on her horse's back. She clung to Sosa's mane until the feeling passed. An arrow grazed the Appaloosa's rump; enraged, he surged forward into a gallop. She pulled back hard on his reins. Snow flew in all directions as the confused Appaloosa came to a haunch- sliding halt. Another arrow hummed by, snagging the sleeve of her blanket coat. Swift Runner reined the little horse around. A Crow was desperately trying to free his sinew bowstring that had become entangled in his horse's mane. He jerked and tugged trying to rip it free as Swift Runner shouted the Lakota war cry, "Hokahey!" and rammed her heels into Sosa's ribs. The spotted, gray Appaloosa lunged forward as though he'd been rump-swatted by a mountain cat.

Although small in stature, in his day, Sosa had been a great war horse. This was unknown to the Crow warrior's horse; all he saw was an enemy horse that was much smaller charging toward him. He surged forward to meet Sosa's attack, almost unseating his master and further throwing him off balance.

As the two mounts narrowed the space between them,

Swift Runner absently noted that the Crow's breath was coming in frosty bursts almost as fast as his pony's. He had given up on his bow; it dangled and flopped about the tangled mane as though alive. As he shouted his Crow challenge, a wicked blade war hawk was brandished overhead; a long triangle of panels of bright beadwork fluttered from the handle.

Sosa's neck stretched out ahead of his driving hooves; bared yellow teeth reached for the Crow horse's vulnerable legs. When the two animals came together with a loud, meaty thud, it was the Crow horse that faltered and staggered backward, dropping to one knee. The smaller horse's attack on its legs had apparently made the larger Crow horse hesitate, slowing just enough to lose his impetus. Both horses' screams of rage and pain reached above the nearby sounds of conflict and fighting.

The Crow fought to regain his balance and tried desperately to swing around in time to use his war hatchet. Beneath the garish war paint, Swift Runner recognized the surprised face of an old friend. Completing a mighty swing, her heavy horn bow caught He Who Rides Alone across the forehead and knocked him from his horse as easily as a throwing stick topples a grouse off a tree limb. The warrior hadn't even hit the ground before the winter air was disturbed by the frightening shout of the Lakota coup cry, "Anho!"

Swift Runner, seeing that her path was clear, urged Sosa into a full gallop. She looked back and, through the clods of snow thrown up by Sosa's hooves, saw her one-time suitor sit up and cradle his head between both hands. Her laughter crackled with joy, splitting the frigid night air and drowning out the fading sound of fighting. She turned her attention to the west where she knew the beginning of the trail to the top of the ridge must start. After her last vision it was obvious that Joshua was at the mountain's crest. Her heart would not allow her to leave her brave horse, vulnerable to predator or Indian, to pursue her husband on foot. Her instincts told her that they would need at least one mount to get clear of the mountains and their enemies. Although closer to him when near the Blackfoot fire, she still thought their chances of surviving were better if they were not afoot. Without consciously thinking about it, she slowed the mountain horse to a canter and kept on the lookout for hidden enemies and the welcome sight of her wolf, Heyoka.

Swift Runner's mind could not dispel the image of the Indian, obviously a youth, on Joshua's back. Unless she was mistaken, his hair style was Lakota. But then, she mused, what would a young Sioux be doing up here? A fleeting thought made her wonder if the Crow youth, Pony Finder, had survived the fight. Shaking off her curiosity, she rode on, eyes ever watchful for enemies and hidden trails. Clouds moved in and obliterated most of the moon's light, causing her to heel-tap the Appaloosa into a faster pace. Her side vision picked up a running shadow as it left the trees. Heyoka, tongue lolling in a wolf's grin, gracefully swooped in close until he ran alongside the galloping horse. The rhythmic plumes of frost drifting and dissipating over the shadowy shoulders were proof that the gliding wolf was a form composed of flesh and blood, yet remained forever Swift Runner's shadow.

# NINETEEN

Joshua glanced toward where Curly Hair slept, curled against the wall of the cave. The light from their small fire licked across his youthful face and wavy hair with tongues of yellow light. The curly hair was something that the mountain man found truly strange. Again, he wondered about the possibility of white blood. Knowing his thoughts were wasted speculation, he looked away and added a small piece of wood to their tiny fire. Joshua smiled as he admitted to himself how good their medicine had been. His biggest worry was, with all the running, what if chance had caused him to sprain, or turn, an ankle like Curly had done. Their fat would surely have been in the fire, he thought.

His thoughts drifted back to just before they had stopped near the top of the ridge. Clouds had moved in making moonlight an on and off thing. Both had been sweating from the exertion of the climb and when they stopped, the cold was relentless as it wormed its way beneath their clothing until it found the damp vulnerable areas. Because of the encroaching cold, by the time they found the cave they had decided to take the chance on a small fire. The cave was L-shaped so they were able to build it away from the front lessening the risk of it being seen. Curly Hair kept watch outside while Joshua built the fire. From his parfleche, Joshua had produced some punk and dried willow bark he'd taken from the underside of a deadfall. Using his flint and steel, it took the mountain man barely any time at all to spark a fire. Fortunately, a dead tree was lying right in front of their natural dwelling, so additional fuel wasn't a problem. He had just finished adding small pieces of wood to the flames when Curly's quiet voice called him outside. Stepping out of the cave, Joshua couldn't see a thing. As his night vision slowly returned, Curly's hiss pulled him in the right direction. But because of the moonless sky, the Lakota was merely a darker form nearby. When he moved closer, the boy's features were more visible. The young Lakota had pointed toward the prairie far below and said, "There, just to the right of that line of pine that looks like a raven's head, there is a small clump of trees. Do you see?"

"I see it, Curly ... another fire." He shook his head, as he added, "It does not appear that they are ready to call it quits, does it?" He looked at the boy and added, "That must have been one special horse you stole."

Curly Hair's grin was a flash of white in the gloom, as he nodded and said, "Yes. He was much horse."

Unexpectedly, orange and yellow lights flashed down below and the popping sound of distant gunfire and war whoops reached their ears. After a few moments it became quiet again. Both were puzzled by the fight down below. After a while they gave up watching and speculating and had retreated to their own fire.

Joshua suddenly tensed. His thoughts instantly returned to the present as he held his breath and listened. All that could be heard was the sibilant whisper of a breeze among the pine. Nothing. Joshua sat back and relaxed but out of habit moved his rifle closer. The moon is covered, he thought, so only four-footed predators should be on the move. The near smokeless fire was of great comfort. Too comfortable, he mused. With the warmth and rest, Joshua could feel his confidence increasing with each passing moment. He didn't want a false confidence making him careless. The cautious thought reminded him that he must soon leave the fire and take a look outside.

His gaze fell once again on the sleeping Lakota. Joshua quietly watched the slow rise and fall of Curly's chest and wondered at the great vitality and stamina that was hidden there. He was pleased that he was getting some much needed sleep. We'll have need of those sharp eyes, he thought, come first light. Joshua studied the peaceful face and smiled. He was always amazed how sleep revealed the innocence that is usually hidden in a young person's expression. He thought how fortunate he and Swift Runner would be if they were to have a son as fine as this lad.

He pulled James Fenimore Cooper's book from the rawhide bag. The flickering orange and yellow fire enriched the battered cover's rugged appearance. He absently caressed the thick leather cover and thought of a time many years past when his father had given him the book. It had opened many doors for him, all leading to adventure and knowledge. He thought briefly of a passage he had memorized long ago, one that certainly fit their situation. Joshua's pale eyes fell on the reclining boy as he whispered the scout Hawk-eye's wise words, "Life is an obligation that friends often owe each other in the wilderness."

He was always surprised how words written so many years earlier could still have a direct meaning in the present. When he saw how difficult it would be to read the small print by their puny fire, he put the book back in the rawhide bag. Besides, he thought, I'd better get busy and think of a way out of this mess. Joshua eased to his feet and slipped by Curly's captured wolf pelt they had hung over the cave's opening. The brisk air invigorated him and seemed to heighten his senses. He was shocked by the display of stars overhead. They were everywhere. He remembered his father saying, 'the stars are the souls of lost lovers eternally roaming the heavens in search of their soul-mates.' He smiled slightly at the sad concept and thought of Swift Runner. He thanked God that she and their unborn baby were safe at the fort. Joshua let his gaze rove down the steep, snow-covered slopes. In the starlit night the trees looked as black as a crow's wing. Suddenly, a harsh truth made itself known to him. His conscience screamed in his ear, "If you can see, they can see!" As panic tried again to get the upper-hand, stories of how adept the Blackfeet were at night fighting flashed through his mind with the speed of heat lightning. They're probably on our trail right now, he thought.

A light touch brought Curly instantly awake and up on his feet. Joshua explained their situation as he collected their belongings and Curly Hair put out their fire. In just moments they were outside and Joshua was again running through the snow. A short time later they crested the ridge. Joshua paused and looked down their back-trail. Nothing moved along the whole length of the starlit slope. The campfire seen earlier was no more. For just an instant he thought of his wife and wondered how she fared. A tiny speck of light out on the prairie winked momentarily and then was gone. He watched for a moment longer; when it didn't reappear he thought maybe he was seeing things. Spinning away from the top of the ridge, he changed his grip on Curly's legs and began running down a snowy, gentle slope. Even with the added weight, Joshua Donner's effortless stride was that of a natural runner. Ahead of them the land opened into a vast, white valley patched with dark pine and numerous other trees.

Curly Hair studied the snowy terrain with knowing eyes. His brief rest had done wonders for the clarity of his thinking. As recognition of the land set in, a wild idea took form with the swiftness of a striking rattlesnake. At that very moment, as they ran across open ground toward a stand of tall pine, the solid ground beneath them vanished. They were falling! Almost instantly they hit solid ground. Curly Hair flew over Joshua's head and landed headfirst in a snowbank.

Their fall occurred because drifting snow had formed a bridge over a dry wash. Fortunately, the empty stream bed was shallow and free of any sizable rocks or deadfalls that could cripple or injure.

Joshua pawed the snow from his face and stared at a grinning Curly. The Lakota youth, spread eagled on his back, had clumps of snow sticking to his face and twisted, wavy hair; he looked like an angry cook had thrown lumps of wet flour at him. The trapper couldn't help but grin, as he asked, "Are you all right?"

Still grinning, Curly scooped the wet snow from his eyes and replied, "Yes." Without so much as taking a breath, he added, "I think I know how we can escape the Blackfeet."

# TWENTY

Dog Killer's rage consumed him. The desire to kill became the most important thing in his future. The disastrous encounter with the Crow raiders was one more thing that the pipe-holder felt was brought on by the Cut-throat pony stealer. Thoughts of revenge danced through his head like demons that would know no rest until they drank the blood of their enemies. A new focus for his hatred had been established with the discovery of the Big Knife who was aiding the Lakota. Knowing that there was no bond of friendship between the Big Knives and the Cut-throats, Dog Killer was puzzled by the actions of the pair he hunted. Why, he wondered, is the Big Knife helping the Cut-throat to escape? From their tracks and from what his warriors had told him, the Big Knife is carrying the pony stealer on his back, as though he were his slave.

Clouds crossing the face of the moon began to slow their tracking. The pipe-holder stopped; those who followed his lead also stopped.

Directly behind Dog Killer was the Blood warrior, Tall Bird, and another Blood named, Elk Heart, who was renowned for his reckless courage. Weasel Fur brought up the rear.

Dog Killer studied the movement of the clouds and

made a decision. He squatted; his warriors also dropped to their haunches. Weasel Fur, who was still favoring his kicked leg, sat instead of squatting. He leaned against a slender aspen which promptly dropped a branch-load of snow down his neck. This action brought several muffled chuckles from his comrades and a murderous look from his leader. Dog Killer captured the attention of all three as he looked at Tall Bird and said, "The night light is about to leave us; before she covers herself I will leave this trail and seek out our war lodge." With mention of the war lodge, Dog Killer gestured toward the top of the ridge above them. Tapping Tall Bird on the chest, he added, "You and your brother will follow the Big Knife's tracks as long as you can. When the tracks can no longer be seen, I will bring you a nose and sharp teeth that will lead us to glory and revenge."

Tall Bird acknowledged the pipe-holder's words with a brusque nod. He cradled his broken arm where he had tied it across his chest and thought of personal glory. In his heart he knew that he would not wait for the Piegan leader, but would push on in hope of catching the enemy himself and gain self-redemption for his earlier failure.

As one, the four Blackfeet rose. Dog Killer gestured toward the one-eyed Weasel Fur as he added with sarcasm, "Since it was I who brought this man who moves through woods with the stealth of a mountain cat ... he will come with me."

White grins on dark faces were the only parting gestures that Weasel Fur received as he sullenly followed the pipe-holder up the side of the slope toward where their war lodge was hidden on top of the ridge.

Tall Bird and Elk Heart wasted no time. Immediately they picked up the pace and began to jog along the swiftly diminishing snow trail as it moved in a diagonal slant rising toward the top of the snow-covered mountain.

Later, Dog Killer and Weasel Fur covered the last of

the ground between them and the war lodge in a darkness that was quickly decreasing. Clouds had shifted and a sprinkle of stars had appeared. As they neared the tipi-like structure, Dog Killer used a bird call that warned of his approach. Both men stared at the dim outline of the primitive dwelling as they awaited a response.

The war lodge was made by staking small trees, long pine boughs, and other assorted branches into a cone-shaped shelter. Sometimes dead tree trunks and other such objects were used to solidify the temporary storage lodge.

Weasel Fur stared at the large animal that stepped into the open. He recognized the form at once. He whispered, "*Makwi* (he who gets and eats plenty)," and brought the wolf/dog's baleful stare focused in on him. The huge, black animal (half wolf and half husky) was a legend among the Piegan. His ferocity and viciousness were only equaled by his master, Wolf Chief.

Weasel Fur's relief was instantaneous when he saw the heavy rawhide lead reaching from the thick, furry neck to the brawny arm of Wolf Chief as he followed his animal into the open. Like his wolf/dog, the warrior was large for his species. Over six feet tall, the Piegan was broad and muscular. His blanket capote made him look even wider. He was hatless and wore his hair in two thick braids. A pair of bedraggled feathers slanted across the back of his large head, while small black eyes glittered cruelly beneath a prominent brow and a broad beak of a nose.

When Dog Killer and Weasel Fur stepped forward, the wolf/dog lunged toward them but was stopped by the muscular arm of Wolf Chief. The animal's savage snarl was answered by a vicious jerk on his lead and an equally feral growl from the throat of the Piegan. Makwi quieted instantly but continued to stare with murderous eyes.

In spite of the chill in the air, Weasel Fur felt sweat bead across his forehead. He stared at the curled lips and

119

long, white teeth of the killer dog and wondered at the malicious ferocity of his fellow tribesmen.

The one-eyed Piegan was not a coward; he was simply a man that believed in 'live and let live' and was more suited for the council fires than for following the war road. His beliefs were unlike his pipe-holder. Dog Killer was a man obsessed with revenge and killing, as were most of the men from his village, and failed to understand anyone who was not the same.

Weasel Fur only half listened as his leader explained to Wolf Chief what was expected of him. Weasel Fur's thoughts of late had been erratic; he couldn't quite focus or become a part of Dog Killer's vengeance quest. When the pipe-holder had invited him along on the war party, he had seen an opportunity to better himself and his family. Because Dog Killer had been somewhat of a friend, he had decided to go along. But never in the past had his friend been so obsessive. After the lost opportunity to acquire the pony stealer and Big Knife's horses, Weasel Fur's interest had waned. At heart, he was not the warrior type. And since the Blackfeet's' main method of attaining wealth was through raiding, the one-eyed Blackfoot in the past had not provided as much as he would have liked for his family.

Still on his braided lead, Makwi led them; Wolf Chief, with an iron grip on the rawhide leash, followed. Dog Killer was next with Weasel Fur bringing up the rear. While trudging through the snow, Weasel Fur dreamed of sitting beside a crackling fire in his warm lodge and playing with his young children. Sitting nearby was his plump wife who watched and smiled at their foolishness. As the plumes of frost passed his lips and nose in rhythmic bursts, a smile showed white on his dark face. With his family waiting at the village, Weasel Fur knew in his heart he had all the wealth he would ever truly need.

Like glittering campfires of the gods a multitude of

stars appeared overhead and lighted their way: two men, and a vicious animal, driven by blood lust, hunted for an elusive enemy. Another man followed, a simple man trying to survive in a world where the weak die young.

# TWENTY-ONE

Sosa moved along the narrow trail like a cat on a tree limb. Swift Runner sat confidently on the small horse's back as the sure-footed horse carefully picked his way along the snowy path. In front of them trotted the ghostly wolf, Heyoka.

The snow-covered ledge slanted across the face of the escarpment like a white scar slashed across the cliff's stone face by an angry creator. Swift Runner's arrows and bow were in their quiver resting across her lower back. Sensing that if she were to meet an enemy on the narrow trail her bow and arrows would be ineffective, she chose to carry her Paterson revolver in hand resting on her lap, her only prayer being that if she did meet an enemy, please Wakan Tanka, let him not be on horseback.

Ever since the fight with the Crow, Sosa Minne had been acting like a horse half his age. It was obvious that the fight with the Crow war horse had left her spotted, four-legged warrior wanting more. Swift Runner knew, without a doubt, that if she came face to face with a mounted enemy there would be no holding the old war horse back. And considering the narrow ledge, they would all probably wind up on the rocks down below.

The stars hovered overhead with the sparkle of a million fireflies. She shivered from the night chill and pulled the lapels of her hooded capote together. The stars reminded her of a summer night several winters ago when the stars were just as bright and they were camped further south beside a shallow ford of the Elk River. She remembered a warm breeze that was just strong enough to keep the mosquitoes and gnats away. It was a time that she would never forget because several things happened, good and bad, that showed her some differences in Joshua's character that she had not seen in a white man before.

The stars overhead filled the whole sky with their happy glitter. A slight breeze rustled the leaves of the cottonwoods nearby and spread the pungent scent of hot, simmering coffee throughout the camp. The metal pot was perched on rocks keeping it partially in the fire. Joshua was sprawled on the other side of the flickering flames studying a familiar object he held on his lap.

He had explained to her long before that what he was doing was called 'reading' and the black marks on the thin skins was known as 'writing.' He had gone on to tell her that he was reading a 'story.' He made the comparison between reading a story and the Lakota storytellers, or the village crier, who was usually a man that periodically wanders through the village and voices the latest news.

Swift Runner covertly watched from the other side of the fire. Her eyes were on her husband while her hands cleaned her weapons. She saw a slight movement of his lips and wondered why. He is as absorbed, she thought, as when he is tracking a deer to fill an empty stomach. How can this be? She was puzzled. Joshua looked up and caught Swift Runner's quizzical look.

"Is something wrong?"

Swift Runner saw the concern in his eyes and was embarrassed.

"No, it is nothing," she said, and looked at the pistol

she had in pieces in front of her. She picked up the gun's barrel and frame and began rubbing a cloth saturated with animal fat across its metal surfaces.

Joshua put his tin cup aside and placed his hand on her knee. She looked up and met his gaze. She felt the warmth of his hand spread through the leather of her leggings. His eyes were soft like the blue of a morning sky. Love was there, hovering in the blue shadows.

"I think you wonder why I find so much to interest me between the pages of a book."

Embarrassed by her husband's intuitive remark, she looked away.

Joshua laughed and squeezed her knee as he said, "I understand. But it is a bad feeling not to 'understand.' Am I right?"

Swift Runner felt the subtle flutter of wings in her chest. Whenever Joshua brought on that special feeling she thought of it as a love bird flapping his wings near her heart, reminding her of the strength of her feelings. She looked up at him, smiled tentatively, and replied, "Yes Joshua, you are right. I would like to know. I wish to know all things that make you happy."

"Waste (Good). Soon, I will teach you to read. But first, I want to read you something from my book. And then we will discuss what the wasichu author, James Fenimore Cooper, meant. Would you like that?"

Slowly, Swift Runner put down the gun's barrel and frame. She sat up straight and said with a grin, "I am ready."

Returning her grin, Joshua flipped through several pages until he found what he wanted. He said, "First I must explain; this is a story about a time almost one hundred winters ago. The white hunter in the story is a man very much like me. His name is Hawk-eye and he lives off the land like the Indian. His closest companions are his adopted father with his son, who are Mohican Indians. The Mohicans and whites were at war with another tribe called Huron. Both these tribes live far to the east, beyond where Wi rises each morning."

Joshua, knowing the passage by heart, put the well-thumbed book aside and continued on, in Lakota.

"This part of the story is where Hawk-eye, the two Mohicans and a soldier friend had a fight with the Hurons. The bad Indians had no heart so they ran, hiding a short distance away. The soldier asked Hawk-eye if he thought the Huron would attack again."

With a brief smile, Joshua sat up. He leaned back on his hands, and said, "I will tell you what Hawk-eye said in Lakota, then I will repeat it in English, as it was written. And I will ask you what he meant by his words."

Warming to the game, Swift Runner smiled and nodded, setting aside the greasy, cleaning cloth.

After translating Hawk-eye's words into Lakota, Joshua had to hold his hand out to stop an eager reply from his wife. He looked away from Swift Runner and spoke the ambiguous sentence in English, as though he was Hawk-eye.

"Do I expect a hungry wolf to satisfy his craving with a mouthful?"

A big grin involuntarily spread across her face as she quickly replied in Lakota, "He is saying ... 'Of course they will attack again, they want our scalps; a hungry wolf would never be satisfied with just a mouthful, he would want it all.' Am I right, Joshua?"

Returning her smile, he answered, "You are correct, *Inipi* (Sweet breath)." Joshua's use of his pet name for Swift Runner brought a softer smile and a tender look. She was about to say something when a nearby voice coming from downwind startled them both.

"Hello the fire! Ain't that what travelin' folk are s'posed ta do when comin' up suddin' like on a camp?"

The voice was promptly followed by the menacing

sound of a gun hammer being cocked. Joshua didn't move. He made eye contact with Swift Runner and she froze also. The voice, he sensed, was too close to take a chance by making a grab for a weapon. Besides, he didn't know if the man was alone.

As if in answer to his thought, he caught movement from the corner of his eye. He slowly turned his head. A mixed blood of nightmare demeanor stepped out of the shadows. He appeared to be half Indian and the other half Negro. Beneath the layers of dirt and grease, he looked young but murderous. He had a large-bore rifle aimed at Joshua's head. Just to the breed's left, the owner of the voice stepped into the light and proved to be just as filthy as his partner. Judging by his dress and sunburned face, he was a white trapper of middle age. His reddened face was dominated by a yellow, evil eye that threatened to pop out of its scabrous socket; the other eye socket was covered with a patch made from something strange, the likes of which he couldn't quite make out. Joshua had never seen the pair before, not during rendezvous, nor any other such doings. He was suddenly filled with apprehension. It had just dawned on him who they must be. He couldn't resist throwing a glance at his wife, wondering if she had guessed their identity.

Deep inside he knew they must be the pair of killers who had been robbing and killing up and down the rivers. There was talk of them at every post or fort where they had stopped. It had been going on for months but mostly on the bigger rivers like the Missouri or the Mississippi. Most of the talk had been how their victims had been mutilated worse than if by Blackfeet.

His mind began to franticly search for a way out. Whether they were the murderers or not, it was obvious that this pair was after their horses, traps, and all their other valuables. Joshua sensed that if he didn't do something soon they would not see another sunrise. He met Swift Runner's gaze, hoping to instill some hope with his look. He knew immediately that it was a wasted thought. She didn't need the vote of confidence as much as he did. Already his wife's eyes glittered with hate and her face had slipped behind its Indian mask. He was certain that her quick, warrior's mind was already at work on how to best kill the two intruders.

The two men moved in closer; the light from their fire gave Swift Runner her first good look at the 'voice.' A snaggle-toothed grin was on the wasichu's filthy face while his single eye peered at her with evil intent. Her composure slipped and her eyes widened in horror when she saw the man's eye-patch. It was a patch of tanned skin that had once been a portion of a woman's breast! The black, shriveled nipple stared at her in lieu of an eye. A tremor ran up Swift Runner's spine as loathing and rage ignited a burning hate deep within her body. Slipping once more behind her mask, she made a silent vow that the monster standing before her would not leave their campsite alive.

Across the fire, Joshua's shocked expression told her that he had also seen the horror. Their eyes locked and without words a bond was formed between them sealing the fate of the two predators.

"Polecat, git our horses."

The evil man was pointing a large Walker Colt revolver at Joshua's head. In his other hand was a big-bore plains rifle. When Polecat moved past Swift Runner to bring in their horses she nearly gagged and understood immediately how he got his name. The breed's leggings were stained near black with dried blood and grease. An uncured scalp of blond hair dangled from his belt.

"Thet be real coffee I smell ... not chicory?"

Neither answered. The one-eyed man slapped the big Colt against Joshua's head. The skin broke open above his left eye and blood, black in the pale light, flowed into his eyebrow.

"When I ask ye somethin', big fella, ye best answer real sudden like."

Only a strong will to live was keeping Swift Runner from killing the savage. She thought she could kill him with her knife before he finished her but wasn't sure. It was best not to do anything until he and Polecat were close by. As it was, the breed could kill them at will from the surrounding darkness. She waited.

Joshua brushed the blood from his eye. He also was waiting.

"Ain't that nice, yer squaw cleanin' yer gun for ye."

Staring straight at Joshua, she felt the brute's eyes crawl over her body like slugs leaving a trail of slime behind. She mentally shivered. He cocked the revolver and held it about six inches from Joshua's head and quietly said, "Don't nobody move now, hear?"

With the muzzle of his rifle he slowly lifted the fringed bottom of Swift Runner's shirt until her breasts were exposed.

Joshua felt a current of violent energy coursing through his veins. Never in his life had he ever wanted to kill a man; he had killed before, yes, but had never relished killing anyone until now. With steadily mounting fury, he silently watched as the monster defiled his wife with his lewd gaze.

His evil eye darted back and forth from Joshua to Swift Runner's naked breasts. His tongue, coated and gray, moved across his dry lips before he said, "Them sure be nice titties ye got there squaw girl."

Swift Runner felt numb. She felt as violated by his eyes as she would have if the monster had actually touched her.

Keeping them both covered with his pistol, he lowered the rifle's muzzle, letting the tanned shirt drop covering her nakedness. He then carefully moved until he was sitting alongside of her, across the fire from Joshua.

Both Joshua and Swift Runner tried not to breathe through their nose; like his partner's, the man's stench was overwhelming.

Behind her, Swift Runner could hear the half-breed bringing the horses. They were wading along the near shore of the shallow river.

"Polecat! Take 'em across the river an' hobble 'em ... then come get these uns' ponies!" he hollered.

Setting his rifle across his lap, the one-eyed trapper reached across the fire and took Joshua's cup of coffee. He kept the revolver pointed straight at Joshua's head until he was once again out of reach. He drained the cup with a loud smacking of lips and with a glance at Swift Runner demanded, "Squaw! More coffee."

She saw Joshua's tiny nod and got slowly to her knees and reached for the simmering pot. The sound of her husband's voice startled her almost as much as what he said. In a fast, low voice, Joshua pinned her with his eyes and repeated the quote from his book.

"Do I expect a hungry wolf will satisfy his craving with a mouthful!"

Joshua's words drew the attention of the monster. As he snarled, "What in the hell you be talkin' 'bout, fella?"

While he spoke, Swift Runner reached for the flame-blackened, coffee pot. She knew exactly what Joshua had meant with the book words. Use the hot coffee ("... satisfy his craving ...") and attack!

"Speak up, or ye're dead!"

With yellow eye staring at Joshua, the monster raised the Walker Colt. Before he could point it, scalding coffee splashed over his head and face. He screamed!

A deafening explosion and a cloud of acrid smoke engulfed them as the Colt discharged. Swift Runner's two-handed swing smashed the heavy pot onto the monster's steaming head! He howled as the coffee grounds slid down his bleeding head onto his face.

Joshua twisted the Colt out of his hand, reversed it, and thumbed the hammer, firing point-blank into the screaming face. The pistol's discharge once again shattered the quiet night. The screaming stopped as the lead ball slammed into the killer, knocking him flat. Before the gun-smoke had time to lift, exposing the dead man's third eye, Joshua leaped over the fire and ran toward the breed that was in the shallows across the narrow river.

Swift Runner spun and lunged toward her bow. She heard the frightened horses snorting and splashing in the water as she quickly snatched her bow and arrows free from their pile of goods.

"Craack!"

The rifle shot brought her head up in time to see Joshua splash into the knee-deep river, apparently unharmed. He stopped and aimed the Colt at the flitting shadow of the breed who was taking cover among the mil-ling horses. He fired. A horse screamed and went down. Joshua stopped; the gun fell unnoticed from his hand into the water. Two other horses scattered away from the flying hooves and splashing water.

Clutching her bow and a pair of arrows, Swift Runner ran forward. She stopped and watched as Joshua, war hawk in hand, surged wildly through the water toward the breed who had managed to slip onto the back of one of the ponies. He had just straightened from grabbing the pony's reins, when Joshua's thrown war hatchet struck him flush alongside the head. The breed reeled in the saddle and grasped a handful of mane to keep from falling. The blade was not firmly lodged in the skull and the war hawk's handle wobbled grotesquely. Swift Runner's arrow ended the half-breed's pain when it pierced his chest and toppled him into the river. Before he hit the water Joshua was already splashing over the stony bottom toward the downed horse. The animal was on its side struggling to rise but was unable to do so.

Notching another arrow, Swift Runner kept her eyes on the downed man. When she saw that he was indeed dead she looked in time to see Joshua reach the horse. She watched as he avoided the slashing hooves and sat down in the water next to the frightened horse's head. The Lakota woman's eyes were everywhere as she searched the starlit river and shore: looking, watching, and making certain that the two killers had been alone. Satisfied, she hurried to join her husband who had managed to scoot his body beneath the horse's massive head and was holding it above water so he wouldn't drown. The bullet hole was right behind the shoulder; she saw the frothy blood coming from the nostrils and knew it was no use. The horse was dying. His struggles had lessoned to the point where he was no longer kicking his legs.

Swift Runner saw a bloody rip in Joshua's linen hunting shirt just above the cloth thrums. The slight wound brought a relieved smile to her lips. On this night, she thought, his medicine has been good.

Joshua cradled the big head and stroked the velvet muzzle with an almost fatherly love. Tears, mixed with blood from the cut over his eye, rolled down his cheeks to disappear into his golden beard. He looked up at Swift Runner, as he explained, "It was an accident. I shouldn't have fired at the breed until the horses were clear." He continued to stroke the long nose and murmur repeatedly, "It was an accident."

Swift Runner quietly waited. She watched her husband with a special pride. In time the animal quieted and seemed at rest from Joshua's soothing efforts. The horse took a final shuddering breath and died. Her husband eased himself free of the great head and carefully removed the bridle, which was a Lakota tradition. He gently lowered the horse's head and allowed it to slip beneath the water. It takes a special man, she thought, to care so much for an animal that was not even his own. Her eyes followed his every move with love and wonder. This man, she thought, is truly a Lakota wearing a white man's skin.

The cloud of frosted breath rose and touched the raised hood of her capote where it disintegrated into feathery tendrils of vapor. As the long night neared the beginning of Wi's journey, the increased cold helped Swift Runner's thoughts return to the present. Her memories reminded her how special Joshua Donner was and increased her resolve to find him. Her mind projected her ahead to where the snowy trail left the cliff face and moved into the forests, icy lakes, and white meadows that lay beyond the summit ... the undisputed land of the dreaded Blackfeet.

# TWENTY-TWO

It was the interim time before dawn when night was its darkest and the cold its most penetrating. Joshua Donner crouched among some snow-covered bushes near the edge of a patch of pine. His focus was to his direct front where a treeless meadow lay before him like a colorless, rumpled blanket. Because of the snow, Joshua was able to see well enough to discern a darker shape if it should appear within the blanket portion of his visibility. Beyond the meadow was another large wooded area that sloped down toward a clearing that encompassed a small lake. Along the shores of the body of water sprawled the Piegan village. Just north of the span of cone-shaped tipis was the Blackfeet pony herd. It was there, among the horses, that Joshua gambled his life on the unknown skills of a fourteen year old Lakota boy.

Curly Hair had convinced the trapper that he could, once again, steal a horse from the Blackfeet pony herd. At first Joshua was completely against the youth's plan, pointing out the obvious, Curly's turned ankle. The young Lakota gave Joshua a quick lesson in horse thievery by pointing out that he had no intention of walking into the enemy pony herd. To steal a horse from an Indian pony herd, he explained, one had to crawl or ride in among them. Curly Hair had further explained, with a winning smile, that since his horse is a prisoner of the dreaded Blackfeet, perhaps he

135

will be happy to rejoin his master. He continued with a tease, saying that Joshua knows first-hand how well he treats his horses.

In spite of Curly Hair's playful manner, Joshua was unable to resist the boy's logic and had agreed. After spending a harrowing interlude of time getting Curly within crawling distance of the herd, the trapper didn't want to jeopardize the boy's chances by staying so close to the village. He thought it wiser to return to the copse of pine where they had left their assorted possessions to wait and agonize over his decision.

Something bothered Joshua, but he wasn't sure what it was. It wasn't the cold; he'd become used to it. His apprehension came from something else. He listened hard, thinking that his subconscious might have heard something that wasn't harmonious with nature and was sending out subtle danger signals…nothing. The trapper's eyes swept the clearing, looking, searching for some small thing that didn't belong. While Joshua's gaze raked the dark meadow and far woods beyond, he felt the nudge of a slight breeze at his back; it tickled where it ruffled his hair near his ears. Suddenly, he caught his breath. Releasing the trapped air in his lungs, Joshua slowly pulled air in through his nose. The sharp tang of cottonwood sap tingled his nose. The short hairs on the back of his neck quivered, sending a tingle of foreboding up his spine. He smothered his telltale, frosty breath with his sleeve and slowly pulled his broad-bladed knife free of its sheath and waited. The mountain man's ears were as pricked as a listening horse's. The remembered fact that Blackfeet used cottonwood sap to destroy their human scent brought a wry smile to his lips. He knew that at least one Blackfoot was nearby. He reasoned that it would be unusual to find cottonwood trees in the mountains. Joshua listened hard and waited. Knowing that when the attack came, he would hear them and he would be ready. Thoughts of Swift Runner and his unborn child tightened his resolve and kindled a fighting rage that, unknown to him, would help him prevail over whatever obstacle he might face.

Realizing that he might be silhouetted against the paler meadow to his front, Joshua slowly eased his big frame lower until he was able to slip behind a nearby bush. He couldn't see a thing within the trees; the darkness was almost absolute. A nearby squeak that came from compressed snow put him flat on his belly. The sting of snow on his hands sharpened his awareness. Rather than put his Hawken in the snow, he eased his rifle into the branches of the bush and pulled his five-shot Paterson from inside his hunting shirt. Knife and pistol in hand, Joshua remained flat on his stomach, eyes glued to his back-trail, and waited.

# TWENTY-THREE

Curly Hair was in among the Blackfeet pony herd. He was crouched beside his own dappled horse, Dust Devil. The warmth that came from his pony's body was welcome in the frigid air. He had already rigged a jaw-lead on him so he was ready to make his approach. By moving in tiny stops and starts, the young Lakota slowly advanced toward a lodge that was positioned near the edge of the herd. The low fire from within made the tipi skins near the bottom of the lodge glow orange, and silhouetted a portion of the guard seated back from the open door flap.

When Curly Hair had first scouted the herd, the night before, he had recognized it for what it was, a place from which the Blackfoot guard could watch the herd. At that time, he had avoided the tipi as though it were infested with the white mans' spotted sickness. That was then ... this time it is different. The owner of the gray horse Curly Hair had stolen was determined it was not going to happen again. He had the herd watcher stake his gray horse directly in front of the lodge's door flap so he would never have the horse out of his sight.

With an almost unearthly patience, Curly Hair worked his way through the Blackfeet herd. After countless stops and motionless interludes, Curly's pony was aligned

139

almost parallel to the black-maned gray.

As the danger intensified his focus was so intense he took every precaution imaginable. Because the frost from his breath could give him away, he would breath as shallow as he could and breathe on his pony's flank or tail.

With a gentle nudge, Curly Hair maneuvered Dust Devil alongside of the gray stallion. At that moment he was very happy that his horse was a gelding. He did not want a squabble between a pair of horses that would be certain to draw attention.

There. Curly Hair breathed a silent sigh of relief as the two horses' noses came together, and they became reacquainted. He stayed very still and allowed the gray stallion to once again get used to his scent. Being careful to keep the ponies' bodies between him and the herd watcher, he covertly watched the painted tipi and the motionless sentry. The lodge was designed in a distinctive Blackfeet style, a wide band of black paint around the base and top, with two rows of perfect white circles painted within the bottom band. Sometimes images were painted on the sides of the lodges indicating a record of their history and tribal relations.

Curly Hair slowly, and oh so softly, moved his hand across the stallion's neck patting and stroking until all nervousness was gone. With a tenderness that was a near caress, Curly slipped the loop of his coiled rawhide rope over the gray's head. In the predawn dimness he imagined, as much as he saw, the stallion's nostrils flare and a big dark eye roll toward him as the stallion gave a brief toss of his dark-maned head. Then it was done. The loop was secured around his head and the big horse calmly awaited whatever came next.

Leading his dappled pony, Curly Hair slowly backed away playing out his long rope as he went. When he felt far enough away he gave some gentle tugs on the rope. The horse looked in his direction but would only take a short step before stopping. Some of the other horses began to slowly mill around which helped hide what he was trying to do. Curly Hair gave a firmer tug. The gray stepped toward him and once again stopped and looked at him. Leaving his own pony, he got on all fours and slowly wove his way through the other horses and carefully approached the gray. The horse watched him come without alarm. Curly froze. It just came to him that there was a change. He could see better now than before. A glance to the east showed that the sky was becoming lighter. His heart began to beat faster as he became aware that time was running out. Keeping the dark shape of the gray between him and the guard's tipi, Curly Hair took a chance and quickened his pace. When he finally drew near, the heat from the gray's body coursed from his hand into his soul. The unexpected sensation lifted his spirit, giving him confidence that his medicine was strong.

His heart nearly stopped when he saw the rope leading from the gray's leg to the lodge. It was no wonder he would not come, he thought, he was tethered from two sides. He took a chance that Wi was not in a hurry and patiently studied the motionless form of the Blackfoot. He waited until he was convinced that the Blackfoot warrior was asleep, then cut the Piegan rope with his knife and slowly eased the gray away from the front of the tipi. His heart gladdened at the sight of another restless horse moving into the space he had vacated. Dust Devil gave a soft nicker as they slowly approached. Without so much as a pause, Curly Hair collected his pony's rawhide lead and led the two from the herd, disappearing into the deeper darkness of the surrounding trees like a Lakota wanagi (spirit). His heart was strong as he moved swiftly through the trees, hoping that he would beat Wi, and especially the Blackfeet revenge raiders, to his wasichu friend.

# TWENTY-FOUR

By back-tracking their own tracks the pipe-holder found the enemy trail easily. Weasel Fur, staying out of reach of the wolf/dog *Makwi's* sharp teeth, watched as Dog Killer pulled cloth remnants from his blanket coat and gave them to Wolf Chief. The big Piegan shoved the rags in front of the dog's nose. Even from where he was standing, Weasel Fur's one eye could see the black stains on the light colored cloth. He knew the black spots must be blood from the Big Knife or the Cut-throat Sioux. The stocky warrior sighed, sensing that the long chase was nearing its end.

The pipe-holder watched as the wolf/dog ripped and tore at the ragged cloth. Wolf Chief's grin and the malicious gleam in his eye made the pipe-holder wish that his enemies were already caught, quivering with fear at his feet. Unconsciously, his fingers caressed the solid shape of his war medicine in the pouch at his hip. With an abrupt signal he waved them onward. Makwi, jerking on his braided tether, lunged up the trail pulling his hulking keeper behind him; Dog Killer followed with Weasel Fur bringing up the rear. With the stars and Night Light gone, the one-eyed warrior was happy to be in the back of the file. He knew that most of the danger would be in the front, but of more importance, with his single eye he could not see well enough to lead. It is well, he thought, I do not need to make more mistakes and have the pipe-holder show more anger toward me.

Through the lingering darkness, they moved like ghosts up the steep trace; only the vapor from their breath validated their earthly presence. The wolf/dog set a pace that was hard to match; even the giant Wolf Chief was hard pressed. Time and again he had to jerk his animal into submission to slow him down.

Following the lean form of his leader, Weasel Fur found himself dreaming of the comforts that awaited him in the village. He imagined holding close the warm plumpness of his wife and thought of the cuddly antics of his young children inside their cozy tipi.

The one-eyed Piegan's random thoughts were brought to an end by the raised arm and loud hiss from Dog Killer. The pipe-holder stopped so abruptly, Weasel Fur couldn't stop before trodding on his moccasined heel. The resulting cuff alongside Weasel Fur's head was a mistake. Had the pipe-holder seen the murderous gleam in Weasel Fur's eye, he would have thought more carefully about the merits of having him at his back while on the trail.

The three Blackfeet crouched beside the snow trail. In the dimness of the false dawn, their blanket capotes, bleached skin leggings, and robes blended magically with the snowy terrain. The motionless wolf/dog, with his blackness, became another bush or small tree. Wolf Chief tightened his grip; Makwi had heard something. They listened. A low, ferocious growl erupted from Makwi's throat before they recognized the noise for what it was. The sound of heavy breathing and the rhythmic squeak of compressed snow grew louder with the steady downward approach of running footfalls.

Makwi lunged forward, breaking free of Wolf Chief's grip! With a terrifying snarl he bounded up the trail.

"AAIIEEE!" The scream brought all three to their feet. Weapons ready, they charged up the trail and stopped almost immediately. The savage, horrible noises coming from the wolf/dog's throat were enough to stop anyone. Makwi was astride someone's chest and was ripping and tearing at the man's throat; blood, black in the gloom, was everywhere!

As Wolf Chief struggled to drag his dog off its victim, Weasel Fur glanced to the east where the sky had begun to spill golden light across the land. He looked back, and shock coursed through his stocky frame causing his knees to wobble and his stomach to churn. The killer wolf/dog had torn out the throat of the Blood warrior, Tall Bird! The warrior's legs quivered then were still. With his broken arm lashed across his chest, the Blood warrior had been unable to protect his vulnerable throat from the killer dog. Weasel Fur noticed that Tall Bird's medicine was no longer tied to his braid. In the weak, diffracted light, the stuffed red bird was nowhere to be seen. He wondered briefly what had brought the Blood warrior running recklessly down his back-trail. Perhaps he had noticed his war medicine was gone and had returned in search of it. Weasel Fur dismissed the thought as useless and with a detached eye watched the pipe-holder who was in animated conversation with the giant, Wolf Chief. With a mental sneer he turned away, thinking them well suited for each other. Sadness came over the one-eyed Piegan. With the addition of daylight, blood could be seen everywhere. To think that the Above Ones had seen fit to have the day's early light expose the unnecessary, bloody savagery of Wolf Chief's killer wolf/dog was like an omen. Seeing the curt gesture from Dog Killer, Weasel Fur could not believe what he was seeing. With Makwi straining at his lead, Wolf Chief and Dog Killer started up the trail. They were leaving their comrade sprawled in the snow just as though it was a

145

discarded body of an enemy.

Whenever possible Blackfeet warriors who are killed on a raid are honored by at least a shallow burial or covered by rocks. In battle, Blackfeet were known to cover their own dead with bodies of their enemy. This was said to 'pay for those who were lost.'

Weasel Fur swallowed his rage at his leader's lack of honor and with a final glance at his ally's abandoned body, followed his leader on his relentless blood trail.

# TWENTY-FIVE

Joshua's eyes tried in vain to pierce the pervading darkness. It was no use; he couldn't see a thing, just hazy, poorly defined shapes. Through the trees to his left, he saw the sky begin to lighten with the coming dawn. At the same time movement caught his eye. His heartbeat quickened. A shadowy figure, briefly silhouetted against the lightening sky, disappeared behind the filigree of branches of a pine deadfall. Joshua's gaze searched everywhere before it returned to his direct front. He had no idea how many Blackfeet were near. The one thing he couldn't afford to do was have enemies coming at him from more than one side. When his relentlessly probing eyes found nothing, he knew he was going to have to take a chance. When the sun crested the horizon, his only ally, darkness, would be gone. He decided to do the one thing his enemy would never expect.

Joshua silently leaped to his feet and ran straight at the man behind the deadfall!

His rapid approach was near soundless as his moccasined feet avoided all obstacles and virtually flew over the snowy ground. All thought of the penetrating early morning cold, like the stiffness in his fingers and legs, left his mind. He was totally focused on the enemy crouched behind the deadfall that wanted to kill him.

147

All at once he saw movement behind the downed tree; his feet left the ground as he dove headfirst into the lattice of snow-covered dead branches.

Wood shattered, snow flew, and branches slapped his face with icy, brittle fingers as he smashed through the fragile barrier! Just before his 200 pounds of taut muscle and bone crashed onto the powerful Blood warrior, Elk Heart, Joshua caught a fleeting glimpse of glittering eyes and light-colored paint dabbed vertically down lean, dark cheeks. A loud grunt, followed by a scream of rage, and Joshua felt unusually hard muscles flex beneath the fringed war shirt. His knife hand was fiercely gripped by a hand with strength equal to his own. Both men were on their knees. With a sudden surge of energy, Joshua slammed the Paterson pistol against the side of the Indian's head. Feeling the Indian's grip lessen, he jerked his knife hand free and thrust toward the man's throat. He missed and a muscular forearm smashed into his face, momentarily stunning him. Joshua swayed as he tried desperately to regain his senses.

The Blood warrior frantically pawed through the snow; he couldn't find his weapon. The brief lapse gave Joshua time to partially recover. Still groggy, Joshua stared at the distorted painted face and felt his knife ripped from his hand. Blood spilling from his nose, the trapper retaliated with a looping right-hand punch that landed on the warrior's jaw. The man reeled, grabbed Joshua by the shirt and staggered to his feet. He raised Joshua's knife and was about to plunge the broad blade down into the favorite kill spot of the Blackfeet, the pregnable space between the clavicle and the neck. Still on his knees, Joshua raised the forgotten Paterson and fired up into the painted face.

The quiet was shattered by the thunderous blast! It echoed through the trees like an electrical thunderclap. The Blood warrior, Elk Heart, stiffened. His legs wobbled and he abruptly collapsed into the bloody snow beside Joshua, where he convulsed, hemorrhaged, and died.

Joshua's eyes, fraught with excitement, searched the trees for more enemies as he scooped snow and attempted to staunch his nosebleed. Light spilled between the trunks of pine and aspen as the sun peeked over the distant hills. Thankful there were no Blackfeet charging out of the trees' long shadows, Joshua quickly retrieved his knife from the dead warrior's fist. He saw that the ball had entered beneath the chin and buried itself in the warrior's brain, killing him instantly.

Joshua quickly dipped a fresh handful of the freezing snow and applied it to his bleeding nose. Knowing the gunshot would bring others; he hurried to his rifle and gathered their other goods. He looked toward the village, praying that Curly had pulled the theft off and was on his way. The golden light spilling across the open, snowy meadow created a sight of astonishing beauty. But for Joshua Donner, it was a vista that could greatly be enhanced by the appearance of a young Lakota warrior riding into the open on a stolen horse.

The empty clearing sent a clear message of impending doom. Knowing that time was running out, Joshua collected everything and moved swiftly into the open. Rifle in one hand, parfleche in the other, he moved straight toward the distant place where he'd hoped to have seen Curly entering the meadow. He was moving slightly downhill; to his left the open ground rose in a snowy incline. The snow-laden tips of pine trees showed above the top of the slope.

While he trudged through the snow, he worried what would happen if he were killed. He wasn't so concerned about 'going under' and losing his hair as he was about what would happen to his wife and unborn child. How would Swift Runner fare without him in this land that was gradually being taken over by the white mans' so-called civilization?

He knew in his heart that it was just a question of time before the Plains Indian way of life became extinct. His fervent hope was that the Indian himself didn't become nonexistent as well.

Joshua stopped. He was hearing something. It was a somewhat familiar sound, but he couldn't place it. It was growing louder. Then he knew; it was panting. The rhythmic breathing of a running animal! He swung around, looking behind. Shock staggered him as surely as if he'd been punched. What he saw was enough to make a brave man run and a drunk sober. One hundred fifty-plus pounds of wolf, or mad dog, was running straight at him and closing fast! Joshua, burdened with the parfleche, extra blanket, and rifle, saw the wide, enraged eyes, the dripping teeth beneath snarling lips and knew he didn't have a chance. Reflex made him try; resolve and tenacity were what saved him.

The parfleche and blanket barely hit the snow before Joshua had swung his Hawken rifle around in front, and managed to lift it parallel to the ground before Makwi's leaping body of solid muscle and bone slammed into him. The force of the wolf/dog's momentum knocked Joshua flat onto his back in the snow. With the rifle barrel braced across the killer dog's throat, it took all of the mountain man's strength to keep the slavering fangs from his throat. The horrifying sounds produced by the dog's fury were wearing Joshua down as quickly as his unbelievable strength. White showed around Makwi's raging eyes as he twisted and lunged, instinctively trying to reach the vulnerable neck. Joshua, needing both hands on the rifle to hold the wolf/dog at bay, was unable to reach for another weapon. Savage, slashing teeth, and fetid breath were gnawing away at his confidence as much as the physical, relentless pressure was sapping his strength. When he saw the braided lead encircling the black haired neck, he knew Blackfeet weren't far behind. It was then he felt his iron resolve begin to ebb away.

From the corner of his eye, Joshua saw a blossoming gray blur of movement; the motion was linked to a snarl that quickly evolved into a roar. The hair-raising sound drowned out the shuddering impact of Heyoka's solid shoulder as it smashed into Makwi, knocking him head over heels into the snow, releasing Joshua from the prison of his weight.

The wolf/dog tumbled, leaped to his feet, and fought back with fiendish determination. Snow and frost vapor were everywhere as Heyoka mercilessly continued his brutal attack and Makwi retaliated with feral relish. White teeth flashed, blood sprayed, and the cacophony of two wild animals savagely ripping and tearing at each other echoed across the snowy meadow. Wolf and wolf/dog tore viciously at each other's throats in a merciless fight to the death.

Joshua had stumbled to his feet and automatically reversed his Hawken. He pulled back the hammer and was ready to fire. While the two animals tore at each other, he stared, completely baffled. His mind refused to accept what he was seeing. Heyoka... his pet wolf, here? How can that be? Forgetting that deadly Blackfeet were probably nearby, he became mesmerized by the fighting animals.

With unmatched ferocity, Heyoka threw the larger wolf/dog onto his back and had his throat before he could recover. The wolf's iron jaws clamped shut, ripped and jerked! Blood sprayed, staining the surrounding snow crimson. Makwi's black form went limp with the light in his raging eyes dimmed and snuffed out. Heyoka gave a final shake and released the dead dog's limp body. Lifting his bloody muzzle, his yellow eyes met Joshua's blue. His broad head turned slightly and his gaze raised, focusing somewhere beyond the mountain man. Still somewhat dazed by it all, Joshua turned and followed Heyoka's line of sight. He stared in absolute disbelief at his wife, Swift Runner, sitting on Sosa and watching him from the top of the snowy incline.

151

# TWENTY-SIX

Swift Runner pulled the Appaloosa to a halt as the golden fingers of Wi reached across the snowy landscape and touched her face and hands. Looking down the slope of the open meadow, she felt a flutter inside as the wings of her love stirred at the sight of her husband standing such a short distance away. A sudden wind ruffled Joshua's long hair and whipped the fringes of his stained and torn hunting shirt. Heyoka, was standing nearby, hovering over an unidentifiable dark mound of fur.

Earlier, when Swift Runner heard the flat report of Joshua's pistol, she rejoiced knowing that chances were good that he was alive. With the gunshot, Heyoka had exploded into motion, disappearing up the incline into the predawn gloom.

Movement at the far stretch of the clearing drew her gaze from Joshua. A rider, leading a large gray stallion with black markings, had just left the trees and was kicking his mount into a gallop, aiming him straight up the hill. Sosa needed no encouragement. Snow flew from his hooves as he burst into an immediate gallop.

Joshua looked. The sight of Curly riding toward him hit him with an overload of joy. He thrilled at the sight of the young Lakota charging up the hill. His wolf-skin was tied at his neck and the fur pelt floated behind him as though alive.

The muffled thunder of Sosa's churning hooves turned him; seeing Swift Runner's warrior gaze zeroed in on Curly Hair startled him into action.

"Heyah! Lakota kola (No! Lakota friend)!" Joshua's shout brought his wife's focus back to him. But only for a second did she slow Sosa. The blood-curdling Sioux war cry, "Hokahey!" leaped from her lips. Her heels pounded Sosa's ribs, and she swept past an astonished Joshua. Through the flying snow he watched her gallop past, swiftly stringing her horn bow as she rode. Then he saw them! Three mounted Blackfeet had left the trees and were in hot pursuit of Curly Hair.

"*Hiii, yii, yii!*" Their war cry slashed across the clearing. Before Joshua had even thought of moving, his Hawken was up, leveled and cocked; he pulled the trigger. There was a resounding, "Craack!"

Through the billowing smoke, Joshua saw the first rider tumble backwards off his hard-driving mount. Quickly, he grabbed his powder horn, pulled the stopper with his teeth, and poured powder down the plains rifle's barrel.

While he worked, his eyes were riveted on his wife as she blew by Curly, who was urging his horses up the incline toward him.

"Boom!" The musket of the closest Piegan discharged a small cloud of blue/gray smoke. Crouched low over Sosa's bobbing head, Swift Runner rode on unharmed.

Patched ball followed the powder; Joshua rammed it home with the ramrod, stuck the hickory rod in the snow.

Curly hauled back on his make-shift reins, as his pony slid to a stop on the slippery, flying snow; he released the stallion's lead at Joshua's feet and spun his pony and raced back down the incline.

Percussion cap firmly in place, Joshua pulled the hammer to full cock. Just as he was about to pull the trigger, he shifted his aim. Swift Runner was in the line of fire!

The two remaining Blackfeet were whipping their horses mercilessly, each wanting to be the first to count coup on the Cut-throat woman warrior.

At the very moment Joshua sighted on the last warrior, Swift Runner reined the Appaloosa hard to the right, a maneuver that put her at a right angle to her enemy and once again blocked the mountain man from his target.

She quickly slipped off Sosa's back onto his side; her left heel was hooked across his haunch and her left arm through a loop in the mane, putting her horse's body between her and the enemy.

Joshua watched helplessly as Swift Runner launched an arrow, and then another, from beneath her running horse's neck. The smart, agile Blackfoot was able to avoid the first shaft, but the second arrow struck him solidly beneath his upraised left arm. He dropped his weapon, grabbed his horse's mane, and struggled to stay on the loping pony.

Swift Runner regained her seat on top of Sosa's back and reined him left in time to see the young Lakota's bow bounce off the head of the wounded Blackfoot, knocking him from his horse. Before the warrior's body hit the ground, she heard the boy's shouted Lakota coup cry, "Anho!" Swift Runner applied heels to ribs and Sosa squatted and broke into an instant gallop, trying to catch up with the Lakota as he closed with the remaining Blackfoot. Before he could do so, the Piegan warrior jerked his rangy paint into an icy skid and turned back. She watched, admiring the young Lakota's courage, as he chased the Blackfoot all the way to the tree-line. Hearing a muffled hoof-beat she turned. Joshua, riding the gray stallion, approached. Swift Runner welcomed him with a smile. Without thinking, she moved Sosa in next to the stallion. The little war horse immediately lashed out with yellow teeth bared and swung around to kick the bigger horse. The big gray arched his neck and did some maneuvering of his own. Swift Runner laughed, quickly moved the Appaloosa out of range, and jumped to the snowy ground. Joshua sprang off his horse, quickly covered the short distance separating them, and swept her into his arms. He stood there in the snowy clearing, face buried in silken hair, and held his wife, oblivious to the fact that more enemy Blackfeet could be near.

With a warm gentleness her enemies would find hard to believe, Swift Runner ran her fingers over the jagged wound across her husband's brow and pulled him closer.

Joshua pulled his head back and stared silently into the black depths of Swift Runner's eyes. Calmness seemed to seep through his body. He no longer felt the cold or the pain throughout his battered body. With a nod toward the approaching Curly Hair, Joshua grinned and said, "I have been thinking. How would you like a son right now... a near-grown son that will prepare you for raising our child?"

Swift Runner stared. Seeing the tease in his eyes, she relaxed and replied, "Are you not tired of carrying this boy on your back?"

The look of wonder on Joshua's face was enough. She knew the tease was over. He will be too busy, she thought, trying to figure out how she knew about his carrying the young Lakota. He had witnessed her gift from the Gods many times, but Swift Runner knew that her husband was always troubled by things he did not understand.

# TWENTY-SEVEN

Dog Killer, Wolf Chief, and Weasel Fur watched from the tree shadows near the edge of the clearing. The pipe-holder's fury was nearly out of control. Seeing that his horse had again been stolen left him trembling with rage. The sight of the Big Knife on his prized stallion had pushed him to the point of wanting to recklessly attack the trio out in the open meadow. He knew his short-barreled musket was no match for the Big Knife's rifle, but his fury was unbearable. Dog Killer lunged toward the clearing, only strides away. Weasel Fur, for some reason, had restrained him and received another backhand blow for his trouble. Weasel Fur's intervention seemed to clear some of the rage from the pipe-holder's head and he calmed down, maintaining a brooding silence.

The hulking Wolf Chief stared intently at the black furry mound lying in the middle of the clearing. Even from where they crouched, they could see the stained snow encompassing the still form. Its only movement came from the wind stirring the thick, black hair. Wolf Chief's lip curled in a silent snarl as he thought of revenge and a bloody fight to the death.

Unseen by the Blackfeet, Heyoka traversed the woods bordering the clearing. Shortly after the killing he had left the meadow to his human masters. His wolf instincts told him that he was to avoid exposing himself in open areas. As always, he lingered nearby, a ghost-like figure floating on the fringe constantly on the lookout for danger and food.

The Blackfeet watched as the three unwelcome intruders gathered their belongings and prepared to leave. A feral growl curled the scarred lip of the pipe-holder as he snarled, "These cowardly enemies will not leave Blackfeet land alive; this I swear."

Weasel Fur wondered at his leader's reason. There had been no sign of cowardice from their enemies; if anything they had showed great bravery. Not for the first time, the one-eyed warrior began to wonder if his pipe-holder's mind was gone.

Dog Killer stood. He gestured for his two remaining warriors to follow him. "Come," he said, "we will pre-pare a trap. With horses, there is only one way off the mountain. We will be waiting for them."

Wolf Chief ignored the pipe-holder and, still kneeling, removed his small pack, then dropped his blanket coat in the snow. His arms were bare; only a vest with the fur turned inside remained on his upper body. Vapor rose from the heated areas of his body. Dog Killer took a step toward him, as he asked, "What are you doing? We must go!"

Wolf Chief refused to be interrupted as he delved into his small parfleche of items. He had scrunched down and his hands were busy. Then he became still; only his arms moved when his head dipped forward.

With the giant's back to them it was hard for Weasel Fur to see what he was doing. With a glance at the clearing he saw that the intruders had begun to walk their horses south toward the distant cliff. In the vast clearing behind them, the dead wolf/dog became a dark island in a sea of white.

Dog Killer was out of patience; he grasped Wolf Chief's shoulder and pulled. The giant Piegan came to his feet and spun around. Both Weasel Fur and Dog Killer took an involuntary step backwards. A tear-shaped drop of wet, red blood ran down the side of Wolf Chief's face. The warrior had gashed both his arms and used his own blood to paint his face for war! He had dipped his hand in blood-paint, cupped his chin, and splayed his bloody fingers across his mouth and up his cheeks.

"I swear I will drink their blood to replace mine and Makwi's," Wolf Chief said. He glared at Dog Killer as he spat out more words of hate and retribution. With a final sneer, he added, "Go. I will seek my own vengeance," and again knelt in the snow and rummaged in his parfleche. Like the pipe-holder, Wolf Chief's world had narrowed to the single anticipation of a blood-letting. Only through spilling the blood of his enemies would the warrior's world be complete and revenge be his.

With the pipe-holder leading the way, they left. Weasel Fur glanced back.

The sun rays filtering through the trees somehow managed to completely miss Wolf Chief. The grieving, revenge-minded warrior still knelt in his small pocket of gloom, totally absorbed in his possessions. Weasel Fur was certain that Wolf Chief's war medicine was what kept him so engrossed in his parfleche. The one-eyed warrior's war medicine was a red-tail hawk foot with a hawk's bell and weasel pelt attached. He carried it close at hand in a pouch on his belt.

Once they cleared the trees and felt the full warmth of the morning sun, Dog Killer broke into a trot, chasing his own shadow. Determined to see his ordeal through to the end, Weasel Fur increased his pace also. Although tired, the morning sun and the crispness of the air invigorated him. He knew in his heart that Dog Killer's ill-fated revenge raid would soon be over, and he would either be dead or on his way home to his loved ones.

# TWENTY-EIGHT

Swift Runner led them. Joshua followed with Curly Hair bringing up the rear. Heyoka was out of sight, ghosting along a trail of his own choosing.

The morning sun pushed their elongated shadows before them as they neared where the trail narrowed before angling down across the rock face of the mountain. Already a rocky ledge had formed on their right and was above eye-level. Snow-capped trees and brush rose above the gray ledge like a green and white topping on a wedge of mottled gray pie. An early morning chill was still in the air, but the warm sunshine proclaimed that a beautiful day lay ahead of them.

Curly Hair was the first to hear the threatening growl. He reined in his pony and quickly began to string his bow as his gaze swept the trees above him. His pony began dancing nervously in reaction to the menacing sound causing him to pause and regain control. A savage snarl followed by a loud thrashing in the underbrush came from directly above.

Joshua and Swift Runner reined their mounts around. Hawken in hand, the trapper rode back to where Curly was deftly handling his skittish pony. The chilling, ferocious sounds coming from the enraged animal were overwhelming. With a flash glance, Joshua saw that Curly was unable to string his bow with one hand. The bushes snapped and shook! Suddenly, the giant form of a naked Indian smeared with blood rose from the shaking underbrush. His hair style proclaimed him to be a Piegan. The Blackfoot's attention was focused on something within the brush and low trees. A large, blurred form hurtled through the air toward the wounded man. Heyoka! For a split-second, Joshua froze! He was mesmerized by the horrible scene.

Heyoka's jaws were clamped in the bunched muscle across the Indian's shoulder. The Blackfoot's hands had latched solidly onto the wolf's neck as if attached there. The big wolf was savagely twisting and squirming trying desperately to break the massive Indian's powerful grip. The warrior was ripped and torn in several places, notably around his huge muscular neck. Blood was flying everywhere; Heyoka's gray hair along his side was sodden with blood. Even as Joshua swung the Hawken into line, the giant Blackfoot ripped the wolf free from his shoulder and raised his twisting, writhing body overhead.

Just as the giant was about to toss Heyoka to the rocks below, Joshua flicked the set trigger and squeezed.

"Craack!" The Hawken bucked; a cloud of smoke briefly enveloped the target. Through the drifting smoke and frost vapor, Joshua saw the frightening figure totter. Abruptly, Heyoka twisted free and half fell from his grasp into the bushes. The Blackfoot's knees wobbled, arms dropped, and he touched the massive hole in his chest. With a loud crash he collapsed backward into the underbrush. Joshua leaped from the gray stallion and began to climb the stony ledge to where Heyoka lay injured. As fast as he was, Swift Runner was quicker. She was already in the bushes crooning soft words in Lakota to the wolf by the time the trapper reached them. After Swift Runner had assured him their wolf would live, Joshua looked at the Blackfoot where he lie sprawled across a dead tree. Clumps of snow had fallen across him from disturbed and broken branches. The snow was rapidly turning to icy red where it absorbed blood from his many wounds. For the first time he noticed that blood had been applied to his face and body as war paint. Through the vapor of his breath, Joshua studied the dead warrior. A small clump of snow had settled onto one of the open black eyes. Gazing at the body, naked except for breech-clout, he thought the warrior must have wanted to fight to the death to satisfy some need for revenge.

A dog-like whimper came from Heyoka where Swift Runner was examining his knife wound.

"Kola!"

Curly's voice drew Joshua to the edge of the ledge. The young Lakota sat his spotted pony and stared at him with concerned eyes.

"Your wolf will live?"

Joshua grinned and nodded.

Curly smiled and said, "That is good. Your wolf saved my life. I would have had no chance against the Blackfoot."

Soundless as a shift in the wind, Swift Runner appeared at Joshua's side. Her beautiful face beamed down at the young Lakota.

"Thank you, Warrior, for my husband's life ... and mine ... for without him, I would have no life."

Curly nodded, smiled in a shy manner, and looked away. Ever cautious, he twisted and looked at their back trail. Satisfied there were no Blackfeet nearby, he grinned up at them. He heel-tapped his pony into a trot. Gesturing at the two horses tied to a rock beside the trail, he said, "Keep the gray, Joshua. He is a fitting horse for a great warrior."

Before Joshua could protest or raise his hand in farewell, the boy had urged his pony into a lope and disappeared around a bend.

# TWENTY-NINE

Muffled by the snow the hoof-beats pounded by on the cliff trail above them. A clod of snow from the passing Cut-throat's horse's hooves actually hit Dog Killer in the face. His rage at having missed ambushing the pony stealer was monumental. His fury was like the great wind when the big snows would come; it seemed to last forever. Dog Killer chastised himself and forced himself to think rationally.

They had taken a treacherous trace along the lower side of the cliff's face to reach where they were, perched on another, smaller ledge just below the main trail. It had been a series of reckless chances taken without the assurance of eventual success. After going through the danger and hardship only to be too late was almost unbearable for the pipe-holder. He rubbed his scarred lip thoughtfully as he struggled to calm himself.

Weasel Fur stood nearby looking over the vista of snow-covered plains spread out below him. He marveled at the work of Napi who had created such a beautiful world for the Blackfeet. Overflowing with benevolence, Weasel Fur even thanked the Above Ones for allowing him to retain the sight of his one eye so that he could still enjoy the wonders of the land. His gaze lifted to the sky, and he saw how the clouds were thinning.

"I do not think the Cut-throat bitch and her dog or the Big Knife have passed yet."

Dog Killer's harsh words broke the one-eyed Blackfoot's reverie.

The pipe-holder continued, "We must move down trail; soon they will be here."

They moved on until they came to a bend in the trail; it was there, on the down side, they placed their ambush. Dog Killer explained that when the enemy rounded the blind corner, they would be waiting. Unexpectedly, he stopped talking. His eyes swiftly searched Weasel Fur's person with barely concealed anger.

"Where is your gun?" he demanded.

Unperturbed, Weasel Fur jerked his head toward the plains as he said, "It was lost when the Blood warriors and I fought the great bear."

"Fought? When you ran is a more probable story," Dog Killer sneered.

Weasel Fur again felt the stirring of anger deep within. His newfound dislike for the pipe-holder was rapidly developing into hatred. Only his respect for his people's custom of giving absolute authority to the pipe-holder, or leader of a raiding party, was keeping him from a violent reprisal.

Dog Killer thrust his musket into Weasel Fur's hands. His black eyes snapped with an obsessive glitter as he remarked, "We must show these outsiders they do not belong in Blackfeet country. When others see the price these have paid for defying us, they will not dare venture into our territory."

The pipe-holder stared hard at Weasel Fur; not liking the lack of fire in his eyes, he snatched the flintlock out of his hands. In doing so, he failed to see that he had brushed the flintlock musket's lock plate against a snow-laden pine branch. A small clump of snow had landed on the gun's powder pan, quickly wetting the fine-grained primer powder. Weasel Fur was about to speak when the pipe-holder made an abrupt gesture, silencing him.

Eyes blazing, Dog Killer proudly proclaimed, "I have changed my mind. I will be the one to confront them on the trail. My revenge should not be dependent upon one who is not quick-witted enough to get out of the way of a runaway elk."

With a scathing look, the pipe-holder turned away from Weasel Fur dismissing him from his mind as he began to apply his war paint.

The one-eyed Piegan thought briefly of the rebuffs, the casual insults, and the embarrassing times he was cuffed like a village cur. He quieted his mounting fury and stood up. Weasel Fur silently turned and walked along the trail they had arrived on without once looking back. While his stocky form moved slowly through the morning shadows, Weasel Fur was careful where he placed his feet. One slip and he knew he could wind up on the rocks far below. He painstakingly avoided the thawed portions of the trail. Very faintly he could hear fragments of the pipe-holder's voice. Thinking Weasel Fur was still close by, the Blackfoot leader had begun speaking again. The voice was too far away to understand his words, but the stocky warrior continued walking until the only sounds he heard were the natural sounds of his beloved wilderness and the creatures that lived in it. The sun was warm on his broad face. Weasel Fur smiled and thought of his family waiting for him in the village. Not once did he feel guilt about not telling Dog Killer that his powder was wet.

# THIRTY

They were still on the narrow cliff-face path so it was necessary to ride single file. Thankfully, the sure-footed Sosa seemed more content after the incident with the Blackfoot. Swift Runner looked back at the small travois being pulled behind the fiery Appaloosa. Heyoka was strapped onto its rawhide platform; his light colored poultice looked white against his dark gray hair. Swift Runner's gaze lifted to be assured that Wakan Tanka had truly returned her husband to her safe and sound. Joshua smiled at her and glanced back, making certain they weren't being pursued by Blackfeet from the village.

Swift Runner carefully scanned the stretch of trees up ahead as she thought of their earlier encounter with the musket wielding Blackfoot.

Being in the lead, she had noticed a sudden increase in the wind. She thought she heard voices. When Swift Runner rounded a sharp bend in the treacherous trail, she jerked her horse to an abrupt stop. A hideously painted Blackfoot wearing a feathered, otter fur hat and a white, black striped, capote was standing in the middle of the narrow trail aiming a short-barreled musket at her. He stood solid as stone. Only his braids and the feathers on his hat moved in the surprisingly strong gust of balmy wind.

Neither Swift Runner nor Joshua moved. Both horses were held firmly in check; the gray was just nervous, but the old war horse strained at the bit. He sensed a forthcoming battle and imagined the scent of spilled blood. It was what he'd been waiting for ever since their encounter with the Crow.

The Blackfoot was less that two arrow lengths in front of Sosa. Swift Runner was baffled, then frightened, by the fury she saw in the man's eyes. Immediate insight told her the man's mind was gone.

At that very instant, Dog Killer had pulled the trigger. After a metallic click, clearly heard in the sudden quiet, nothing happened! As the baffled, totally enraged Blackfoot shook his musket in distress, Swift Runner released Sosa's tightly held reins. The aging war horse lunged forward. Vapor exploded from Sosa's mouth and nostrils as his bared yellow teeth reached for the painted warrior!

Seeing his own rage mirrored in the spotted horse's eyes, the pipe-holder's quick reflexes were his undoing. He dropped his musket and leaped aside. He teetered on the brink of the cliff only long enough for his hand to close over his war medicine, the carved effigy of a war horse. He fell silently into the void, his mind scrambled by the cruel irony until his life ended on the rocks far below.

All thoughts of the murderous Blackfoot left Swift Runner's mind as the trail suddenly widened. They had arrived at the bottom of the cliff. The timbered, snow-covered land sloped gently downward toward the sweeping prairie. She listened to the wind, heard the rustle of the slender branches among the birch and aspen. A song bird began a lilting melody that made her long for her unborn child. The hiss of the travois' poles traversing through the snow was a tuneless lullaby that made her think of running water and the shush of a mother's lips.

Joshua brought his spirited stallion up alongside the

Appaloosa, but not too close. The feisty little horse was keeping a close eye on the larger gray. The trapper looked at the blue, cloudless sky overhead and was amazed at the difference a day could make. He looked south at the pine, birch and aspen-covered hills and thought of his cabin where his storage of prime pelts awaited his return. Joshua knew they weren't enough to last them through the summer and following winter as he had wished, but for the moment he was simply glad to be alive. He exchanged a loving glance with Swift Runner and cautiously looked behind and to the sides making sure no Blackfeet were lurking nearby. He let his thoughts drift and inevitably they turned to their unborn child and his unbelievably brave wife. As the land began to flatten and open up into a gentle incline of low, rolling hills, Joshua covertly slowed his mount just enough to allow him to watch Swift Runner without her being aware.

With her hood down, the sun brought out reddish highlights in her ebony hair. An unseasonably warm breeze lifted raven strands and whipped them across her coppery brow. The lingering winter chill had painted a rosy hue to her cheeks, emphasizing the high cheek bones and healthy sheen of her skin.

Swift Runner felt Joshua's eyes and turned, meeting his gaze. Joshua blushed as though he were a schoolboy caught in the act of some unseemly thought. Swift Runner laughed.

To Joshua's ears the musical sound was like the tinkle of ice-covered pine boughs brushing against each other in the wind.

With a mischievous look, she said, "If you do not stop looking at me with the eyes of a love-sick, rutting moose, we might not make it to the warmth and comfort of your cabin."

Joshua laughed and thought how good his medicine had been. He joined Swift Runner in her constant survey of the land as they once again rode side by side. His stomach growled reminding him of how little he had eaten in the past day and night. The half-formed scabs across his brow began to burn and itch. At least, he thought, my headaches are mostly a thing of the past.

An errant breath of wind stirred a nearby aspen; the slim branches rubbed together making subtle scratching sounds. For some unknown reason hearing the wind murmur and rattle among the trees made Joshua think once more of the future and how they would fare in the months to come. I'll think of some way, he thought, to earn enough to winter with my family. He was determined never to leave his wife alone, ever again. She had told him of Jed Smith and what she had been forced to do. Even knowing the man was dead, Joshua felt a simmering anger that wouldn't leave; it burned in his stomach as though waiting to be turned loose. Perhaps because of his anger, he thought it best that they didn't return to Fort Whitewater. You never know, he thought, how some whites might react over the death of one of their own by the hand of an Indian. Frontier hatreds ran long and deep, and with her red skin Joshua knew it was a fifty/fifty chance whether or not there would be trouble, even if she was right in protecting herself.

Joshua buried his anger and lifted his face to the warmth of the sun. A balmy breeze added to his pleasure, while he breathed in the crisp air and thought of spring.

# THIRTY-ONE

Swift Runner was listening to the wind; it was talking to her. The song birds were no longer singing. Up ahead an eagle that was circling suddenly stopped and flew back toward the mountain. Her gaze dropped. A white man was leaning against a tree aiming a rifle at her. She hissed a warning at Joshua and pulled Sosa to a stop. Eyes riveted on the man with the rifle, she heard Joshua stop the gray beside her. The heavily accented voice came from directly behind them.

"*Hola*! Welcome, red whore! Did you no forget to say, adieu? After you murdered our frien' did you thin' we would let you jus' ride away?"

The sound of Frenchy's voice behind them was like gunpowder added to Joshua's simmering anger. He fought down the rising rage and remained absolutely still. The sound of footsteps trudging through the snow was making the hair stand up on the back of Joshua's neck. He waited.

"Both step down from horses. *Mon ami*, Donner. If you move quick, I kill her, eh?"

His French accent added to Joshua's horror. He didn't understand. Did Frenchy want him to hurry, or not to hurry? Before he dared move, he softly said, "Frenchy?"

"*Oui?*"

"You want me to move slow, or fast?"

"You, by damn, better not be quick! I blow hole through red bitch!"

With his side vision, Joshua saw that Swift Runner was dismounting as slowly he was. With sinking heart, he eyed the brass and wood stock of his rifle tied to his saddle, while thoughts of his revolver buried beneath his heavy winter coat made him sick with guilt. He got caught like some 'pilgrim' who was still wet behind the ears.

"Zeke! Come to here, mon ami!" Frenchy's voice seemed to echo in the stillness of the mountain slope.

"Put hands up an' turn to me."

Swift Runner faced the friend and partner of Jed Smith. The sight of the little man's unwashed skin and greasy buckskins made her feel unwashed herself. Even his red knit cap was greasy and stained. Most of his sun burnished, grizzled face was covered with an unruly black beard. It gave credence to her peoples' habit of calling wasichus 'hair mouths.' A burning hatred that seemed to start at her very core and spread through her body like the ripples in a pool made her want to scream in fury at her helplessness. Inside her capote she felt the hard metal of the Paterson pressed against her belly. Her unstrung bow and quiver of arrows hung useless across her narrow back. These wasichus, she thought, were going to kill her and her child. Her husband ... he too would die, unless she did something.

Joshua watched Frenchy closely. He could hear the approach of Deke as he lumbered through the snow. Frenchy's black eyes were darting here and there like a pair of water bugs trapped inside his skull. Think, damn you, or you're going to die in the snow like a cow slaughtered for meat. His desperate thought was interrupted by the arrival of the big trapper, Deke. The long fringe on his grease blackened elk-skins swished with each stride as though he

174

were walking through a field of tall grass instead of melting snow. He strode up to Frenchy and shoved him hard, as he angrily said, "Ya damn papist, Frenchy. How many times I gotta tell ya ... it's Deke! Not Zeke!"

Frenchy's eyes flashed and he abruptly pointed his big-bore plains rifle at Deke.

"You no push me, Zeke ... I kill you, quick!"

While a frightened Deke stuttered and put his hands out in front of him, as though holding his partner at bay, Joshua was able to sneak a step closer to them. One of Deke's hands was wrapped in a stained, bloody cloth that was nearly as filthy as he was; the other held his rifle.

"Now, Frenchy," Deke whined, "I din't mean nothin', honest!"

Joshua saw Deke's eyes slide past Frenchy and fasten onto the travois. His face turned crimson with rage. He forgot the Frenchman's rifle and lunged forward.

"The wolf! He has returned to me ... I'll cut his black heart out!" he raged.

His bandaged hand went to his wide belt and jerked his knife free as he loomed over Heyoka, helplessly strapped onto the travois platform. Knife hand poised, Deke leaned forward.

From the corner of his eye, Joshua saw the brave wolf's head lift and heard his snarl of defiance. The rest became a blur as his leap carried him forward and his fist smashed into the larger man's jaw. Deke staggered backward; his knife slashed across Joshua's chest, ripping through his leather shirt. Before the murderous trapper could pull back, Joshua had grasped his bandaged knife hand and squeezed. Deke screamed! The knife dropped into the snow.

"A-ah!"

Swift Runner's warning brought his head up and around. He was staring into the large muzzle of Frenchy's .50 plains rifle. Behind the huge, round opening Joshua saw the water bug eyes dancing a devil's jig. He saw the hammer fall as he threw himself to the side.

"Craack!" The explosion deafened him! As Joshua fell back through the ensuing fire and smoke, he saw Swift Runner's hands flash behind her neck, then one hand swiftly hurtled forward. In the eerie silence he saw her knife flicker once then bury itself in Frenchy's narrow chest. Shock momentarily kept the Frenchman upright, where he quivered and shook. The absence of sound made the scene even more horrible for Joshua; clouds of breath vapor, flying blood, violent movement, and sudden action gave it all a macabre, unreal feeling.

Movement above him and to his right had him fumbling for his war hawk stuck behind his belt. He was lying on it! As he struggled to free his hawk, he helplessly watched the silent tableau develop before his horrified eyes. Deke had swung his rifle around and was lined up on Swift Runner but was having trouble pulling the hammer back with his injured hand. Warrior that she was, Swift Runner had rushed forward and knocked the dying Frenchman to the snowy ground. As she struggled to free her knife from his bony chest, Joshua swung his freed war hawk and struck Deke behind the knee. A plume of breath vapor exploded from Deke's gaping mouth in a silent scream and he collapsed onto his back like a felled tree. Suddenly, Swift Runner was there and her knife was in Deke's throat before he could take a last breath.

Joshua got to his knees and swayed like a sapling in the wind. He smelled something burning. Swift Runner, face stern with concentration rushed over and began slapping his face with a mittened hand. He grabbed her wrist. She grinned and her lips moved. He couldn't quite hear what she was saying. He stumbled to his feet and began working his jaw back and forth. His hearing slowly returned in time to hear his wife say, "... was burning."

"What did you say?"

Swift Runner grinned again and said, "Your beard was on fire. It will give me reason to shave you."

While Joshua was digesting her words and separating them from the ringing in his ears, Swift Runner quickly strung her bow while her gaze made a sweeping survey of the surrounding terrain.

Joshua got to his feet. His hand went to his head which had started to ache. He avoided looking at the two trappers. I've seen enough death and killing, he mused, to last me a month of Sundays. He saw that their horses had spooked and moved off a bit. Joshua walked through the snow toward them as though he'd been swinging an axe all day. All the expended energy of the last two days was catching up to him. Heyoka and Sosa watched him come.

The wolf's yellow eyes watched Joshua's every move as he carefully untied the lashings that held him on the travois. He watched as Heyoka slowly and gingerly climbed off the hide platform. Joshua thought, he moves exactly like I feel.

Joshua watched Heyoka move stiffly through the snow, gradually loosening his sore muscles. Joshua moved to the gray stallion and removed his rifle. Still embarrassed by being caught like a greenhorn, he looked everywhere, especially their back trail for anything that didn't fit, or harmonize, with nature. Satisfied, Joshua looked back at Swift Runner who was collecting the two trappers' valuables. He smiled as he remembered that at least one of the two plains rifles was a Hawken. Should fetch a fair price at summer rendezvous, he mused. But we're still a far piece from getting that stake we need. Joshua shrugged off their future needs knowing that he had plenty of time to think of something.

"Their horses are in yonder patch of birch; I'll get them!"

Swift Runner raised her head and waved at his call.

When Joshua stepped into the cool shadows of the copse of birch he was surprised to see a pack mule standing with the trappers' horses.

"How come they need a mule," he asked himself, "to go along with their horses?"

Stepping up to the mule, the gray animal rolled his eye and watched Joshua's every move. "Stand still long ears, I don't aim to hurt you," he murmured. The mule was loaded down with everything imaginable. Looks like they weren't planning on going back to the fort after the killing, he thought.

A pair of heavy appearing leather bags strung over the fork of the pack-saddle caught his eye. Opening one, a shaft of sunlight made him blink as it bounced off one of the objects inside the bag. Gold coin! Joshua stared, half afraid to believe what his eyes were telling him. He looked in the other bag ... same thing! At first he couldn't understand how two such sorry specimens of mankind could wind up with all that gold.

For years there had been rumors that Smith, Frenchy, and Deke had been moving around Indian country selling their rot-gut, watered down whiskey to the Indians. They probably had *plews* (prime beaver furs) and other furs cached in several places. Their trips to Santa Fe and Taos were where they exchanged their furs for gold coin.

That could account for part of it, he reasoned, but not all. Still thinking, Joshua moved out of the trees into the open. Swift Runner was by the horses cleaning an arrow with snow. Bandage still in place, Heyoka was nearby eating a rabbit. Swift Runner saw Joshua watching and waved.

"I will be there soon," he said. While he watched her dry, then replace the arrow in its quiver, he thought of last fall. Then he knew.

Joshua quickly moved back to the mule and removed

the two heavy bags, weighing them in his hands. He remembered last fall when the last keel boat of the season, on its way to Fort Whitewater, had turned up missing; all hands on board had disappeared as well. When he thought of all the supplies on board that could have been sold, he realized that they must have been the ones responsible. Joshua shook his head and wondered at the cold-blooded minds it took to do the thieving and killing. They were a lot smarter than they looked, he mused. They hoarded it all, and by not spending much never drew any attention to themselves.

Joshua slung the bags of coins around his neck by their connecting thong and grabbed the horses' reins. Tugging on the mule's lead, he moved into the sunlight. He got a perverse enjoyment from the weight of the gold hanging from his neck, but by the time he reached Swift Runner's side he was happy to sling the bags over the fork of Sosa's saddle.

Already mounted, Swift Runner looked perplexed as she gazed down at his beaming face.

The balmy wind blew tresses of ebony hair across her tawny countenance and created a picture of beauty and love that made Joshua's happiness complete.

With concern shining from midnight eyes, Swift Runner asked, "Why do you smile so, my husband?"

He tried hard to quit smiling, but when he thought of their child safe and happy in sunny Taos and festive Santa Fe, he couldn't stop.

# CHEYENNE, WYOMING
## JULY 4, 1886

The old marshal's eyes sparkled with delight as he watched the boys' pleased reaction to the end of his story. All the boys but Wes McBride began talking to each other in excited voices. Sensing that he wasn't finished, Wes continued to watch the old marshal.

Movement pulled the marshal's gaze toward the dusty sprawl of Sixteenth Street, as he added, "Curly Hair rode east to hook up with his people, while Swift Runner and Joshua moved on south toward Taos and Santa Fe."

Wes followed the old marshal's line of sight and noticed three riders walking their horses down the middle of the street. Except for a couple of dust devils there was no other movement the entire length of the thoroughfare. Not finding much in the three horsemen to interest him, Wes tugged at the old man's sleeve as he asked, "Did Joshua ever see Curly again?"

The marshal, seeing four sets of eyes and eight pricked ears waiting expectantly, brought his attention back to the boys as he replied, "Yessir, he did. It was back in the summer of '67, over at Fort Laramie. At the time, the trapper was working for the army as an interpreter. They had some peace talks going on then with the Sioux."

Wes noticed how, in the shadow beneath the wide brim of his hat, the marshal's eyes shifted and followed the riders as they moved on past. Two of the men were wearing linen dusters and the third was dressed in a suit a lot like the marshal's, only his hat was a dude's narrow-brimmed affair. He wondered briefly if maybe the two wearing dusters were a bit soft-brained, wearing dusters in the Fourth of July heat. Wes put it out of his mind and looked up at the marshal, whose gaze was still following the riders.

"Did they talk to each other?" Wes' question brought the marshal's regard back to his young audience. The redhead noticed how the marshal's big mustache gave a little twitch as he smiled at him and said, "Yes, they did, Wes, but not for too long. Curly Hair was an established warrior by then and was a pretty serious fellow. His people had become his whole life. Hating the soldiers the way he did, Curly didn't have much to do with those that worked for them."

Johnny, the towhead, asked, "How come I ain't never heard o' him before?"

"Yeah, Marshal. How come?" Wes added.

The marshal grinned and stood up. He reached out with his weathered hand and playfully ruffled Wes' mop of red hair as he said, "Oh, you heard of him. You see, 'Curly' was his boyhood name. His grown-up name was Crazy Horse."

Wes felt as though someone had socked him in the belly. All four boys looked at each other in disbelief and then back at the marshal who was again staring up the street. The boys all began talking to each other at the same time. The marshal turned and pointed a gnarled finger at them and in a stern voice said, "You boys stay right here. Don't go in the street. If I see you there I'll wale on your bottoms."

Four sets of eyes, still big with wonder and surprise at the true identity of Curly, stared as the marshal turned and walked away. Wes looked at his friends, jumped to his feet, and exclaimed, "You heard the marshal, stay put! I'll be right back."

Wes left his friends sitting with gaping mouths. With a hop and a skip, he hurried along the boardwalk to follow in the marshal's dusty wake. The marshal had left the boardwalk and was walking in the dirt along its edge between the hitching rails and the street. Beyond the marshal, Wes saw the three strangers rein in across the street right in front of the First National Bank. The one wearing the dude hat stepped down from his horse. He was carrying a pair of saddle-bags as he walked up to the bank door and rapped on the fancy window. The second fella climbed down off his horse.

Wes was watching so close he tripped over a loose board and nearly fell; when he looked up again the man was going inside. How come, he wondered. The bank's supposed to be closed Independence Day. He watched as the second fella, one wearing a duster, followed the first inside the bank. Wes stayed on the boardwalk and watched the old marshal duck beneath a hitching rail and step into the dusty street. The third rider, also wearing a duster, stayed on his horse. Wes noticed that his horse, a line-backed dun, was skittish. A small tumbleweed blew on by his nose and set the dun to prancing here and there. The marshal continued his approach, unseen by the rider who was busy calming his mount. Wes, spellbound, slipped behind a water barrel and watched.

The marshal kept his eyes pinned on the rider. He noticed how the stranger kept one hand inside the pocket of his buttoned duster, relying on the other hand to handle his spooky dun. Still advancing, the marshal slipped his right hand inside his coat and pulled a long-barreled Colt from its shoulder rig hidden beneath his arm. The marshal's pale gaze jumped back and forth between the bank door and the lone rider. By the time the rider had calmed his mount, the marshal was close enough to see the expression on the man's unshaven, sweating face.

When he saw the old man, with the tin badge peeking from behind his coat, the rider threw a glance at the bank door, faced the marshal, and smiled. The marshal stopped and returned the smile, keeping his body between the rider and his hidden right hand, which held the pistol.

"How do." With his words, the marshal assumed a relaxed position; his weight shifted to his right leg while his hands went to his hips, the gun hand still out of sight.

"Howdy right back at ya, Old-timer."

The man on the horse punctuated his reply by spitting a gob of tobacco juice near the marshal's feet.

From the boardwalk Wes' eyes were nearly bugging out of his head. He didn't know for sure what was going on, but he knew there was going to be big trouble. The marshal looked relaxed, but the big Colt dangling from the marshal's hand said otherwise. Wes waited. With the gun out of sight of the man on the horse, he didn't know what to expect. What did happen was a sight he knew he would never forget.

A sudden gust of wind swept a swirl of dust into the heated atmosphere. The marshal, eyes hidden in the shade from his hat, saw the door to the bank begin to open from the inside. Smiling sheepishly up at the rider, he pulled his hat off with his left hand exposing a shock of gray hair. He wiped the sweat from his brow on his sleeve as he said, "Too damn hot ... for a bank robbery."

At his last startling words the marshal skimmed his hat under the nose of the skittish dun and screamed exactly like an enraged mountain lion, "YEEOW!"

With the threatening hat, combined with the feral scream, the line-back dun exploded, leaping upwards into the dust-filled air!

Wes watched as the surprised rider almost left his saddle. Buttons popped as the duster blew open exposing a double-barreled shotgun clutched in the rider's right hand. The twin muzzles swung toward the marshal. The marshal's big Colt barked once; dust flew from the punctured duster. The rider grimaced with pain, dropped the scattergun and tumbled from his saddle like a sack of potatoes. The spooked yellow horse screamed and ran up the street, while the other two horses at the hitching rail reared and whinnied, jerking at their tied reins. Wes stared with unbelieving eyes as the old marshal, moving like a much younger man, spun around. Another smaller pistol had appeared in his other hand like magic as he ran toward the bank.

The bank's front door burst open and the other duster-attired rider stumbled into the open, thumbing shots from his revolver. The marshal continued to run straight at him, firing both pistols as fast as he could fire. The rider was hammered back against the brick wall of the bank where he slid to a sitting position and died, coughing blood into the dirt. Wes, eyes popping from his head, watched as the marshal slid to a stop. He turned sideways to the bank and raised the big Colt as though he were shooting at tin cans down by Crow Creek. Just as he leveled the big revolver, Wes saw the fella wearing the dude hat step through the bank doors and slip into the open. He was carrying bulging saddle-bags in one hand and a pistol in the other. The marshal's Colt spit a tongue of flame and the bank robber spun to his left and collapsed into the dust. The marshal kept his gun aimed at the downed robber until he was still. An errant puff of wind swept the marshal's grey hair off his brow as he turned and walked back toward the first man he'd shot. Wes stared so hard he thought his eyes were going to cross. He couldn't believe what he was seeing.

A gunshot, loud in the sudden quiet, rang out! The marshal staggered back. Wes' mind screamed, 'He's been hit!' The marshal raised the Colt and fired once. The outlaw that had been shot off his horse jerked from the impact of the bullet. He was lying belly down in the street, revolver still leveled toward the marshal. The outlaw lowered his pistol and seemed to grow smaller as he drooled blood into the sand. His face dropped onto the patch of dirt darkened by his blood. He shuddered and died. The dead outlaw's sprawled form was unexpectedly encompassed by swirling dust.

The marshal took a step forward, stumbled backward, and sat down. Wes was suddenly on his feet. People ran from nearby buildings but stopped at the edge of the street; they appeared frightened to step into an arena where life-ending violence had occurred. Wes ran into the street, dropped to his knees beside the marshal, and stared. The old marshal was sitting in the dirt of Sixteenth Street, calmly punching empty shell casings from his Colt and reloading. He pinned Wes with his faded blue eyes as he said, "Wes, when I heard them footsteps coming behind me I knew it was you. You've got grit, boy. I'm proud of you."

Wes couldn't answer. His gaze kept jumping from the long, jagged purple scar across the marshal's pale forehead to the ragged, size .44 hole in the left breast of his suit coat. Wes stared, waiting for a river of blood to abruptly gush out and for Marshal Joshua Donner to fall over dead. The marshal winced as he slid the long-barreled Colt back in its holster. The smaller pistol disappeared beneath the coat flap on the right side.

"I think I might of cracked me a rib," he said. The old marshal held a hand up to Wes and added, "Help me up, Son. I want to be on my feet before I get trampled by all our brave citizens."

Wes noticed how the town folks were cautiously moving into the dusty street. Several voices were raised, asking the marshal if he was alright. Wes, still stunned by what he had witnessed and discovered, stared in awe as the old marshal raised his hands and assured everyone that he was fine. Wes' mind was turning cartwheels. How can he be fine, he thought, he was shot plumb center; I saw the entry hole right over his heart.

Someone handed the marshal his hat; everyone seemed to be talking at once. Wes stood in the street dazzled by it all, oblivious to the increasing wind and the milling crowd of people. Suddenly, the old marshal was standing in front of him. Wes saw him flinch and grimace with pain as he bent from the waist. With his face only inches away, the marshal placed something heavy in Wes' hand. His gaze held Wes' as he said, "I want you to have this, Son; there's messages in there that'll help you grow. Next time you have any doings with Indians, remember ... they're just folks, same as you and me."

The old marshal looked much older as he painfully straightened and began fussing with his hat. Wes realized this was the first time he ever saw the marshal without his hat on. He looked down at the battered, leather bound book in his hand. The title, The Last Of The Mohicans, was almost completely worn away by age. Only a portion of the author's name was there; the rest had been obliterated by a bullet hole. Wes stared and saw the dull gray sheen from the lead bullet lodged, deep within the pocket-size volume's thick pages. Wes looked up. The marshal was turning to leave. City folk were throwing questions at him left and right; he nodded at one, waved off another.

"Marshal Donner?" The question in Wes' voice stopped the marshal in his tracks. He waved off the others who were still talking to him and turned and faced the youngster. It was as though he had been expecting more from Wes and was resigned to deal with it.

Wes was almost afraid to ask but knew that he had to know.

"What about her, Marshal ... your wife, Swift Runner. Where's she at?"

The marshal met Wes' gaze, blinked, and turned his

head. As was his habit, he looked west, up Sixteenth Street and beyond to the jagged, purple line of mountains. Wind pushed a small cloud of dust that swiftly enveloped them and passed on before dispersing into the bright blue sky.

The marshal looked at Wes, then pawed briefly at his eyes to dislodge some dust that had apparently lingered there. His voice, when it came, sounded distant and was husk with emotion

"Well, Son… that's … another time, another story."

The marshal slowly turned, and with his hand pressed against his lower left chest, gingerly walked away.

Movement caught Wes' eye and he saw his three friends running into the street toward him. Looking away, his gaze was again drawn to the tall, aging figure of Marshal Joshua Donner as he slowly walked through the whirling plumes of dust toward the stairway where Doc Phillip's shingle swung from its rusty chains.

The End

# AUTHOR'S NOTE

Extensive research was done to make the time and place in <u>White Horse, Red Rider</u> as realistic as possible. The streets and buildings in 1886, Cheyenne, were carefully researched. My many thanks go to the assistance from the historical society and museum in Cheyenne, Wyoming. Some liberties were taken with the location of individual businesses to be cohesive with the story-line.

In researching the Blackfeet, I found no reference they trained dogs to track or hunt man.

All the characters in my book are fictitious with the exception of the young, Tashunke Witke, who, as an adult became a charismatic leader of the Oglala Sioux. His involvement in my story is a figment of my imagination.